DEATH LORD

CLAIMED BY LUCIFER BOOK FOUR

ELIZABETH BRIGGS

DEATH LORD (CLAIMED BY LUCIFER #4)

Copyright © 2022 by Elizabeth Briggs

Cover designed by Sylvia Frost, thebookbrander.com

1

BELIAL

In New Orleans, very little separated the living from the dead. Tombs sat above ground in the dozens of cemeteries across the city, where visitors left daily offerings to appease the restless spirits. Songs of the dead echoed through the French Quarter, telling the story of the city's violent, tragic past. Tourists flocked to ghost tours and combed abandoned buildings, hoping to get a glimpse of the supernatural.

If only they knew how close Death truly was.

From the rooftops, I watched my prey move through the alleys below, blending into the darkness almost perfectly. The only thing that gave him away were the scuffs of his shoes along the pavement, and the occasional flicker of his shadow over a lighter patch of alley.

I followed along the edge of the building above him without making a sound, my form cloaked in darkness. He carried on, unaware that he was being stalked by something far worse than him. Death was already in the air—I could taste it on my tongue like a familiar, intoxicating drink. It grew stronger by the minute, and I knew I'd only have so much time before I'd have to act. Because *he* would act soon.

My stomach clenched, empty and wanting. Unnatural hunger burned inside me, a pounding need that had to be fulfilled. I had to feed soon...or else.

The man stopped in a patch of light and I got my first good look at him. He was on the shorter side for a modern-day male, with tawny hair that looked messy and a long nose that defined his face. He glanced around as if checking to make sure he was still alone, but he never thought to look up, still oblivious to the danger above him. He had no idea that Death stalked the streets of New Orleans alongside him, searching for the next doomed soul to consume.

He slid into an alley with intermittent, flickering lights, where a shape slumped against the wall. The shape stirred and croaked out words too quiet for me to hear. A dirty hand came up, peeking out of blankets, asking for a handout. The man I'd been following sneered and towered over the helpless human, and I knew it was time.

I jumped across the rooftop to the next building, landing softly. The tang of magic filled the air as the man changed into a large bobcat, revealing his true nature as a shifter—a type of demon representing the sin of wrath. He snarled and the human screamed, trying to get away as the bobcat readied to pounce, fangs bared.

I dropped down from the roof in a swirl of darkness, my cloak fluttering behind me, my hood concealing my face. I landed directly between the shifter and the human, just as the bobcat lunged. I knocked him back with a blast of darkness, and he hit the wall on the other side of the alley with a sickening crack. But that wasn't enough to kill a shifter. He recovered fast, back leg lifted in a limp, and his eyes widened at the sight of me—and then he ran.

Of course he did.

Disgust curled my lip. This was the third person he'd attacked in as many days, but this time I was here to stop him before he left another body behind.

I summoned Ghost, my horse, who appeared out of the shadows, bowing his pale head as he approached. I mounted him easily and we took off after the bobcat, racing down the dark alleys across cobblestones and cement, a mix of new and old. A rush of adrenaline flowed through my veins at the chase, and the promise of what was to come—because there was no escaping Death.

In his panic, the shifter ran into a dead end, and I cornered him against a wall. As I leaped off of Ghost's back, the shifter returned to his human form in a swirl of magic. I gestured for Ghost to vanish again as I stalked toward my prey.

"No..." he muttered, his eyes wide as he looked up at me. "It's you..."

"I see my reputation precedes me," I said in a low voice.

"Please, spare me," he gasped out.

"Like you were going to spare that man back there?" My hand snaked out of my cloak to grab hold of the shifter's throat and I lifted him up in the air. "I think not."

At my touch, life began draining from the shifter into me. He choked, scrabbling uselessly at my arm as I tightened my grip. His power flowed into me, sating that deep, aching hunger that plagued me constantly. I closed my eyes and breathed in deeply, relishing the brief moment of peace.

Something cold and painful plunged into my back, and I jerked my head to look over my shoulder. An ice spear protruded from my cloak. *What the fuck?*

I dropped the bobcat shifter, who collapsed onto the ground in a heap, too weak to do anything for the moment. Whoever had interrupted my feeding was going to pay for it.

I reached around and grasped the spear, gritting my teeth as I pulled it out of my shoulder and shattered it in my hand. When I looked in the direction of where the spear must have come from, I spotted a woman standing about twenty feet away. My breath caught as we locked gazes, not only because she was gorgeous, but because her pale blue eyes burned with a deep, fiery hatred that contradicted her icy powers. Pure white hair flowed down her back, and she wore all black leather that looked like it was made for combat. She lifted her hands up and magic hummed in the air as her ice hit me like a brick wall. I brushed it aside with a flick of power, and she bared her teeth, her fingers lengthening into claws.

Great, another shifter. These two must be working together, which meant they both had to die. Fine with me. My appetite was insatiable and I could feed all night long, especially if it meant getting other murderers off my streets.

As she threw another blast of ice at me, the bobcat

shifter took the moment to dart away. Damn it. I'd have to hunt him down again after I drained this one of life.

"You're going to regret that," I said as I enveloped the shifter in thick, inky darkness. She struggled as it wrapped her limbs tight to her body until she could hardly breathe. She let out a gasp, her bright eyes flaring as she looked at me defiantly. She didn't seem scared.

You will be, I thought with satisfaction as I stalked forward, tightening my darkness around her in slight increments. She'd already ruined my hunt, so I didn't mind making her suffer just a little bit before I drained her of life. She struggled harder, seeming intent on getting away from me. She bared her canines as I drew closer, trying to bite my hand as it lifted toward her.

"Don't worry, it will all be over soon," I said as I wrapped my hand around her throat. Our eyes locked and I was struck again by her beauty, even as my fingers tightened on her soft, delicate skin. A shame to kill one so lovely, but if she was working with the bobcat shifter then she deserved this fate.

I began to drain her of life...but nothing happened.

Something was different. It took me a few heartbeats to realize I didn't feel the overwhelming need to feed anymore. For once, I wasn't absolutely starving for life.

Instead, I felt a different type of hunger. Like lust, but stronger. I wanted to devour her, but in a completely different way than usual. My thumb brushed against her pulse, which was beating rapidly, and my gaze fell to her lips. I had a sudden desire to pull her closer and claim her mouth with a rough kiss. Or to throw her over my shoulder and carry her back to my bar, where I'd spread her legs and feast on her pussy.

My hunger for death had been replaced—by a hunger for *her*.

2

EIRA

Belial tossed me to the ground as if I'd scalded his hand and he couldn't let go of me fast enough. I landed hard on the dirty cement and clutched my neck, drawing a deep breath into my aching, burning lungs. He could have killed me easily, just like his other victims—so why had he stopped? And what was that weird sensation I'd felt when he'd touched me? Something that felt...*right*. Even with his hand around my neck, choking the life out of me. Which made zero fucking sense.

I looked up at the man the press called the Grim Reaper of New Orleans as I tried to catch my breath. Belial's tall, muscular frame towered above me, and his presence bled into the space outside of the physical bounds of his body, taking up more room than he had any right to. He wore a black cloak with a hood that completely hid his face, though I'd caught a glimpse of his hard eyes and chiseled jaw when he'd stared at my mouth like he'd been about to kiss me. Another thing that made no sense.

"Who are you?" he asked in a low, dangerous voice.

Anger flared inside me at the sound. He was the reason shifters had been going missing all around the city. He was also my father's killer. I had to stop him at all costs.

"I am vengeance." As soon as the words left my mouth I launched myself upwards, shifting mid-lunge into a huge white wolf, my claws and fangs crystallizing into lethal ice.

But he dodged my attack easily, moving so quickly I almost missed it. I twisted and tried to attack again, but he simply maneuvered away in the blink of an eye once more. No matter how much I attacked, he didn't fight back, but simply stared at me. I couldn't see his expression, but I got the impression he was studying me, or perhaps sizing me up. Like a specimen laid out under a microscope, bright lights trained on me and a giant eye watching my every move.

I shifted back into my human form and threw multiple shards of ice at him in quick succession. He didn't dodge this time, but simply raised a hand up. Blue flame lit in his hand, melting the ice, and I froze at the sight—*hellfire*. Only Belial and his father Lucifer possessed such a deadly power, and if it hit me, this would all be over.

Was that how he'd killed my father?

My anger flared once more, burning deep in my stomach, and I let out a yell as I rushed Belial. I formed an ice sword in each hand and swung them around, preparing to attack. He formed a sword made of darkness and easily parried my attacks, as if my years of combat training was nothing against him. Damn it! What would it take to kill this asshole?

I raised my swords to strike again, but a rush of dark power rolled out of Belial in a wave. My jaw fell open as something burst through the cement at my feet—a bony white hand. A choked scream escaped me as more hands reached up all around me, grabbing for my boots and anything else they could use for leverage. I could only gape in horror as freaking *skeletons* started crawling out of the ground, moving closer with jerky movements like something out of a nightmare.

Belial only looked on as bony fingers reached for me. I chopped and dodged, but the skeletons were relentless and their undead hands wrapped around my upper arms, holding me firmly in place. I gritted my teeth, unsure how I was going to get out of this alive, as I conjured shards of ice, but they did little against the skeletons surrounding me.

Belial stalked forward as I struggled against the skeletons, but there was no escaping them. He drew close enough for me to get another glance at his annoyingly handsome face under that dark hood. My chest clenched, and not entirely from fear.

Don't get distracted, I chided myself. *He's the son of Lucifer, of course he'd be devastatingly sexy. He's also going to fucking kill you.*

I lashed out with my ice magic, trying to make one last-ditch effort to get away. Finally, some of the control the skeletons had shifted slightly, and I shoved at that with all my might, my heart thundering in my chest. I scrabbled with the tiny bit of freedom I'd won, throwing everything I had against it. If I was going to die tonight, I was going to fight against Belial as much as I could.

But it wasn't enough.

Belial grabbed my arms with impossible strength and speed, snapping a pair of silver cuffs on my wrists.

"What are you doing?" I cried, as I looked down at them, trying to jerk my hands away. The instant they were on, I felt hollow—like my magic had been stripped away completely. I tried to call my wolf, or summon my ice magic, but it was like a cage surrounded me, preventing me from accessing my powers.

With a sinking sensation, I realized I recognized these silver cuffs. I'd seen them on prisoners of the fae during my time in Faerie, and they blocked all magical powers, basically turning the person wearing them into a regular human. I'd never experienced them before, and after feeling my magic blocked from me like this, I never wanted to feel it again. But why was he doing this instead of simply killing me, like he'd almost done to that other shifter?

The skeletons disappeared, fading to dust all around us. Belial didn't need them anymore, since there was nothing I could do to get out of the cuffs. I could *run* though. I glanced around, looking for the best escape route.

"Don't even think about running," Belial said, with that low, hard voice, as tendrils of darkness snaked around me, trapping my arms at my sides.

"Let me go, asshole!" I shouted, trying to summon my anger again, along with my courage. "Or at least have the balls to kill me already!"

Belial's eyebrow arched at that, and then a tendril of darkness snaked its way up my neck and sealed itself across my lips. I screamed against it, struggling harder, but it held tight. There was nothing I could do but glare at Belial, trying to relay exactly how I felt about him through my eyes.

"I'm not going to kill you," he said. "At least, not yet."

"Why not?" I asked, but it came out a garble of repressed, furious sounds.

"You're coming with me."

He scooped me up into his strong arms as my muffled protests got louder and more frantic. I struggled with everything I had, but between the cuffs and his shadow bindings, there was nothing I could do. Besides, he was way too powerful, much more so than I'd expected.

He cradled me in his arms like he was rescuing me, as his huge wings snapped out behind him. They were impossibly beautiful—his feathers inky black at the top, then fading to gray, then turning to white along the bottom tips. I'd be impressed, if I wasn't being kidnapped.

With a sweep of his wings, we lifted into the air. My eyes nearly bulged out of their sockets as we flew higher, while shadows swirled around us, blending us into the night. If I had access to my hands, I would cling to him for dear life. As the twinkling lights of New Orleans zipped beneath us, I prayed he wouldn't drop me. Then again, maybe I'd be better off if he did. A quick death, rather than whatever he had in mind for me.

Where the hell was Belial taking me—and why?

3

EIRA

Belial's feet finally touched down on the roof of a building in the French Quarter, and I let out a long breath, my muscles relaxing slightly. Was flying across the city amazing? Yes. Was it terrifying? Also yes.

I still had no idea where the Grim Reaper of New Orleans was taking me either. Was he going to torture me? As part fae and part demon, I healed faster than any human, although that wouldn't be true with these damn silver cuffs on. I struggled again for good measure as Belial walked toward a door on the roof, but he didn't even seem to notice my efforts.

He threw the door open and stomped inside, narrowly smacking my head against the door frame. I snapped, "Watch it," but the stupid shadow muzzle on my mouth turned it into gibberish. This asshole was getting an earful when he finally took it off me.

The stairwell inside was nearly pitch black, but my

demon eyes let me see well enough in it. Not that there was much to see as we went down three flights to another door. Belial threw this one open too, and I craned my neck to look around. We were in a basement with no windows, filled with bottles and barrels of alcohol, cleaning supplies, crates of snack food, some bar stools, napkins, and table cloths, and a refrigerator. Had he taken me to his bar? I'd been watching it for a few days before I'd made my move against him, trying to learn his habits and his schedule. That was how I'd known he would go out tonight...to hunt.

I'd given up struggling at this point, and I didn't even try to yank at the darkness as Belial finally set me down. It was obviously futile. He had me in the magic-draining silver cuffs, and his own magic was airtight. I was sure he could hold me like this for as long as he needed. All I could do was glare up at him and hope he combusted on the spot from the hatred searing in my veins.

He dropped me in a heap in the corner of the room on the dirty floor, and I let loose another stream of swear words he couldn't understand. I fell silent when the clink of metal against metal met my ears. My fears were confirmed a moment later when Belial pulled chains out from a cabinet and started toward me with them. I scrambled back, my bound feet trying to catch footing and failing, and then my back hit a wall. I was well and truly trapped here with this psychopath who seemed impossible to kill.

Belial let the chains drag along the floor as he cornered me at the wall. He released the darkness cocooning my wrists, but only to snap a chain to the silver cuffs. I watched helplessly as he attached the other end to a hook on the wall. I didn't bother tugging on it. The chain was thick enough that I'd almost call it overkill.

He quickly searched me all over, presumably for other weapons, his hands roaming across my body over my combat leathers. I froze as he touched me, and even though there wasn't anything sexual about it, my breath hitched anyway at how near he was. He found no weapons, but did confiscate my phone, the bastard. Then he reached into a cabinet and pulled out another set of silver cuffs.

"No!" I cried out through my muffle. I strained against the length of the chain, trying to get away from him, but there was nowhere to run and no way to escape. He captured one foot and held it tight so I couldn't kick him as he attached the cuff around my ankle, and then quickly slapped the other one on before I could try to kick him again. He added another chain to those cuffs, and attached it to the same wall hook. Why did he need a wall hook? Did he keep many prisoners down here? Fuck, what kind of sick bastard was he?

Belial stepped back to admire his handiwork. I glared at him, hating him with every fiber of my being. He waved his hand and the pressure sealing my mouth shut vanished. Finally.

"Let me go, you fucking psychopath!" I snapped instantly.

He arched a dark eyebrow. "Now why would I do that when I just got you here?"

A tremor of fear ran down my spine but I refused to let it show on my face. "What are you going to do to me?"

"I haven't decided yet." He leaned against a stack of crates, crossing his arms, and observed me. His dark gaze wandered over me in a long, lazy roll, and then came back up to my eyes. He smirked as if he'd just seen something incredibly funny. "Tell me who you are... or better yet, what you are."

I debated not telling him a single thing. But then, what was the point in hiding it? He already had me chained up, and he could probably torture the information out of me if he needed to. "My name is Eira, and I'm the daughter of Fenrir."

Understanding flickered across his face, so slight that I would have missed it if I wasn't watching so closely for his reaction. "Is that why you're here to kill me?" He sounded almost amused. "Revenge for your father's death?"

"That's not the only reason," I growled.

I hadn't been at the battle in Hell where my father had been killed, but my older brothers were there and they'd told me everything. Sure, my father had fought a war against Lucifer, but it was Lucifer's eldest son who'd dealt the killing blow. My father had made many mistakes, but I'd loved him anyway, and I couldn't forgive Belial for his death. Even so, I hadn't planned to go after him until shifters started going missing or turning up dead all around New Orleans, and when my brothers came to investigate, they disappeared too. The media had called the "vigilante" the Grim Reaper of New Orleans, mentioning how he only killed criminals, rapists, and others the police never caught, but I knew what he truly was—a murderer who had to be stopped.

"Where are my brothers?" I asked. "Have you killed them?"

"I have no idea what you're talking about," Belial said.

"Liar! You've been killing off shifters in this city, and even more have gone missing. Did you bring them down here before killing them? Is that what you're going to do to me?"

He snorted. "You're the first I've chained up down here in many years."

"Wow, I'm honored," I said, my voice dripping with sarcasm. "How about you free me and we finish what we started in that alley"

"Are you so quick to go to your death?" He smirked, looking haughty and amused and way too fucking handsome for his own good. "We both know you can't kill me. After all, I am Death."

"What are you talking about?" I asked, shock running over me like a bucket of ice water.

Belial just shook his head. "You want to kill me because of Fenrir's death when you don't even know the whole story."

"No, I want to kill you because you're a murderer and you have to be stopped. The trail of bodies you've left across the city is proof. Just like the shifter you were about to murder tonight."

Belial let out a sarcastic laugh. "Is that what you think? I was only attacking that shifter because he was going to kill that homeless man. He's killed many over the last few days, and I'd finally tracked him down and was about to stop him —when you attacked me."

"I didn't see any homeless guy." I'd watched Belial from the shadows as he'd jumped down and grabbed the shifter by the throat, completely unprovoked. "Just you and the shifter."

"I don't give a fuck if you don't believe me," he said, as he tore off his cloak and tossed it aside, giving me a better view of his large, muscular body. "But over the last few months, crime has been increasing in New Orleans, and most of it has come from shifters. I'm only protecting my city, taking out the criminals that can't be stopped by the police. Can you imagine a human police officer going up against a shifter? It would be carnage."

"Why didn't you kill me, then?"

Belial's mood shifted in an instant. He'd been resonating a low-level threatening aura this whole time, setting my teeth on edge and making my hair stand on end, but it suddenly intensified. He didn't so much as move, but something shifted in the air. "That's a good question."

Before I could say anything else, he rushed forward and grabbed my throat.

4

BELIAL

I'd thought that it was just a fluke, but when I wrapped my hand around Eira's throat again, there wasn't so much as a flicker of hunger.

Ever since I'd become Death, I'd been completely insatiable. It had changed me as a person, and I didn't like who I was becoming. My need to steal life was all-consuming, and on some nights I could hardly control it, like trying to contain a hurricane with my bare hands most days. All I could do was direct it toward the evil in the city, taking out the other murderers to hopefully spare other lives. If I had to kill, I would protect the city I loved at the same time.

But the moment I touched Eira, it all changed. The raging and howling in my head for the death of every living thing around me quieted, as if I'd snuffed it out like a candle. I tightened my grip around her throat and tried to drain the life from her. I sucked and sucked, but I couldn't draw a single drop of life from her.

I leaned closer, letting go of her throat and drew in a deep, long breath. She smelled like shifter and fae, a rare hybrid for sure, but nothing that would explain my unusual reaction to her. Beyond the lack of hunger, there was an incredible pull I felt toward her, and nothing I could do to slow it down or halt it. I *wanted* her. Badly.

"Why?" I murmured, only half-aware of what I was saying, as I breathed in her wonderful scent. "Why are you special?"

Eira didn't answer. She was holding perfectly still, possibly with fear, or maybe just as caught up in this as I was. I opened my mouth to ask her something else, but then she drew in a deep breath and slammed her head into me as hard as she could. She jerked her limbs against me all at once, trying to push me away, or topple me over so she could escape, but it didn't do any good. She had no idea who she was up against.

I gripped her chin and shoved her head against the wall so she couldn't move. I smiled, amused that she was still fighting me. Somehow she thought that she could actually kill Death.

"You think you can get away so easily?" I asked, enjoying the feel of her so close to me. I wasn't sure why I'd brought her here, I'd just known I couldn't let her go—not until I learned more.

"I was hoping you'd be distracted," Eira growled.

"Keep trying," I said, as I caressed her chin with my fingers, pressing my body against hers. I couldn't stop myself. I needed to be closer. "Who knows, maybe someday you'll manage to beat me."

"Or you could just let me go," she asked, her voice disgusted. But I noticed she didn't try to fight me again, and she leaned into me too, like she couldn't help herself. She inhaled sharply and her eyes dropped to my mouth, and I spotted desire flickering across her face. She wanted me too, despite her fear and her hatred. What the fuck was happening to us?

And it only got worse with proximity. I could hardly hold myself from back from nosing along her exposed neck, from tasting the sharp beat of her heart and her soft, smooth skin. I wanted to *bite* her, to consume whatever part of her was so alluring just to make it *stop*. Or maybe the only solution was to taste her somewhere else, like between her thighs, before I plunged my cock into her. I grew hard just thinking about how much I needed that. Needed *her*.

"What do you want from me?" Eira asked breathlessly, breaking the spell. I blinked, realizing that I'd nearly pressed my mouth to her neck, and I pulled back slightly so I could look her in the eye.

I didn't have a good answer for her. There was no reason for me to keep her, except that I couldn't let her go. For one thing, she wanted to kill me, and I didn't want to have to pull ice spears out of my back all the time. But that wasn't why I'd really brought her here. I had to find out why she was different, why I couldn't drain her life, and why she soothed the raging hunger inside me for death...and awakened another kind of hunger. Then, once I figured out what the hell this thing was between us, I could stop it. The last thing I needed was a distraction.

If I was smart, I'd pull back and leave her to stew for a bit, and maybe that would cool her awful temper so she could talk to me in a calmer state. But when I looked at her, the overwhelming urge to kiss her washed over me. Lust, I could understand, but this was deeper. I wanted to *devour* her. How long had it been since I'd felt that particular urge?

Eira's pupils dilated like she felt it as well, and she licked her lips. My eyes fell to the movement, and I swallowed, my mouth suddenly, inexplicably dry. She wanted this, too, that much was clear in her eyes, and for a moment, I felt like we were both on the same page. Everything else faded into the background, and all that mattered was the need to seal my lips to hers. Would they taste as sweet as they looked?

No. I couldn't. I was Death, and there was no way I could get involved with anyone. I could kill with just a touch now, and it didn't matter that this particular urge didn't apply to Eira. She was from a different world, and I didn't need to drag her into mine in such an intimate way.

I stepped back and tried to regain control over myself. The want had a keen edge that wasn't going away, and I had to battle against it in an entirely different way from the usual hunger for death. It was dangerous, and I shouldn't tempt whatever it was.

But I couldn't let Eira go either.

She was glaring at me again, her beautiful face filled with hatred. No matter what strange desire drew us together, she still blamed me entirely for her father's death, and that wasn't going to be something that we could get past with a kiss or even a good fuck. But I needed to know why and how she affected me this way, and I had to keep her close long enough for that. I had no doubts that if I left her tied up in my bar's basement, she'd find a way to get out, but there were other options. It was just a matter of convincing her to go for them.

"I've noticed shifters going missing, too," I said finally. "It's not because of me though. Yes, I'm going after the ones who are dangerous and are killing humans, because they need to be stopped. But the others? I have no idea what's happening to them, and I'd like to find out. Maybe it's tied to the increase in violent crime over the last few months." I leaned back against the fridge, keeping my distance from her as much as I could. "Why don't we work together to find out why the shifters are going missing?"

"You want to work...together?" she asked, like I'd just said the most ridiculous thing she'd ever heard in her life.

"Yes. That is, if you can stop trying to kill me for a while."

Eira tilted her head back and shot daggers at me with her cold eyes. "I'm not sure if I can resist the urge."

"I assure you, it's completely futile. I *cannot* die, and it doesn't matter how many ice spears you throw at my back. It does hurt though, and kind of puts a damper on the idea of us working together." I shrugged casually. "The other option is that I can just leave you chained up down here, and go do it myself. I can't have you interfering with my work. Either you stay out of my way, under lock and key, or you work with me. Which one is it going to be?"

"That's really not an option," Eira said, twisting her sexy little mouth up into a scowl.

"At least I'm giving you the choice," I said. "Anyone less generous might have taken offense to you repeatedly attacking me."

"Fine," Eira spat. "I'll work with you, and I'll do my very best to try and not kill you."

She still had that defiant tilt to her head, like she expected me to revoke the offer because of her attitude. *If this was any other circumstance, I'd tease back,* I thought. She was just my type, gorgeous and smart and feisty as a hellcat, but I had no time for any sort of feelings. Right now, all there was, was the mission.

I stepped forward and unhooked the chains from her wrists and ankles. I crouched down in front of her and carefully undid the cuffs on her feet so that she could walk properly. I half expected her to try and kick me and escape, but apparently somehow I'd convinced her that fighting and running wasn't the best idea.

She might just be biding her time to find another escape route, but I hoped I'd be able to show her that I was willing to help her out. There was clearly more going on than what she was telling me. She had seemed very emotional about the shifters going missing, which made sense if she was looking for her brothers, whoever they were. Hopefully that desire to find them overruled her other desire to kill me, at least for a little while.

As I was pulling away from her leg, my fingers slid against the exposed skin of her ankle. Something crackled in the air between us. I wanted to lean in and lick her skin, but I steeled myself and let her go. But I stood up slowly, still caught in her spell. Touching her was intoxicating, and I couldn't get enough.

Eira was looking at me, eyes wide, cheeks flushed. I slid my hand along her neck, and she let out a long breath as her body trembled slightly. Her eyelids fluttered shut like she was going to give in, and she swayed toward me. I let out a harsh gasp, fighting desperately for control, as my mouth drew closer to hers with every second.

I drew back sharply. I couldn't do this. She hated me, and I had no business trying to seduce her. We'd just agreed to not kill each other, for fuck's sake.

No, I'd have to simply suffer through it. I turned away and started up the stairs without waiting to see if she would follow me.

5

EIRA

I looked down at my wrists once more to make sure they were actually freed from the wall. Had Belial really let me go? The silver cuffs still blocked me from using my powers, so it wasn't true freedom, but it was something. I looked around for a weapon to use against him, but all I saw were bottles of alcohol and an old mop. I grabbed the closest bottle of wine I could find and scrambled to follow Belial up the stairs.

I couldn't believe the turn of events over the last few minutes. I'd gone from thinking I was going to die, to agreeing to work with my father's murderer, who was supposedly trying to help the city, even though I'd watched him attempt to kill a shifter in cold blood.

And then there was that weird, crazy desire I felt whenever he was near, which I was desperately trying not to think about. Every time he touched me it was like fireworks were being set off all throughout my body, and intense need filled my core, demanding I touch him back. Or worse, kiss him. No way was I ever doing that, so my body needed to calm the fuck down already.

"Are you ever going to take these cuffs off?" I asked, holding my hands up. The silver caught the dull light and winked. It was excruciating to be cut off from my magic and so powerless. I wondered if this was what it felt like to be human. No wonder they needed so much protection.

"I will when you can be trusted to not stab me in the back with a spear of ice."

"Wow, you're really hung up on that, aren't you?" I sighed. "So, basically...never. How am I supposed to help you if I'm cuffed? I can't use any of my magic or shift at all. I could fall down these stairs and die because I can't catch myself."

He snorted. "I have faith in your ability to walk up a flight of stairs. Although I could carry you, if you're so worried."

The thought of Belial taking me in his strong arms again sent a shiver of lust and fear through me. "Keep your hands off me," I snapped.

Except my traitorous body secretly wanted him to touch me all over, for some dumb reason. Back in the basement, I'd been so sure that Belial had been about to kiss me, and the weirdest thing was that I'd been about to *let* him. My body wanted me to get close to him, telling me I could lean into him, close my eyes, and trust he would protect me, which made no sense at all. Why would my survival instincts be misfiring so hard when it came to Belial? I had never had them fail me like this before. In fact, I'd always prided myself on being able to trust my instincts and be right about a person. But now? Belial was just pulling up a bunch of question marks along with this strange desire that pulled us together like magnets.

I kept having to remind myself that he was the enemy, and that turning my back to him would be like laying myself out in front of a target and begging to be hit. I'd only agreed to help him because I wanted to figure out what had happened to those shifters he'd claimed he hadn't killed, including my brothers. If I stuck with him for a bit, I was sure I'd be able to uncover the truth of what was going on.

I'd also use the time to try and figure out how to kill him. He'd said he was Death, but I wasn't entirely convinced, or even really sure what that meant. Even if he was Death, there had to be a way to kill him. I'd start looking for his weaknesses and how to exploit them in my favor. No one was infallible, and I'd figure out what made Lucifer's son tick—and then use that to end him.

Belial led us through another door and into the bar he owned. I'd only seen it from the outside, where it sat on the corner of a street in the French Quarter, with blue shutters on tall windows and big red doors at the entrance, along with a sign that said Outcast Bar with two black wings on it. Inside, the bar was a mix of new and old, like it had been around for decades but was also managing to keep up with the modern era. Without my shifter senses my nose felt clogged up, but I could still smell alcohol and food in the air, something like burgers and fries maybe.

Along the back wall was a huge mirror with many different bottles of alcohol, and behind the bar was a beautiful woman with Asian features and long black hair, who was polishing some glasses. She wore a black corset that was half leather and half lace and showed off all her assets.

"I just closed up for the night," she said, hardly glancing up as Belial sat down at the bar.

I followed him a bit more slowly, glancing around and noticing that the place was mostly empty, with only a few stragglers hanging around. Of course, he wouldn't want to bring me to his bar when it was open. It would be too easy for me to slip away in a full crowd of people, magic-dampening cuffs or not.

"Surely you can spare the owner of this establishment a drink?" Belial asked.

"For you, sure. But what about your guest?" The woman shot me a brief glance, like I was barely worth her time.

"She needs one, too," he said. "She tried to kill me."

I gaped at him. Who would go around telling people that?

The bartender gave me a second, more appraising glance, and then shook her head and let out a laugh. "Okay, yeah, she deserves a drink."

"Actually, I'll take care of the drinks," Belial said. "Your shift is done. Go home, Yumi."

Yumi hesitated, looking at me again. This time, I saw a small flicker of worry in her gaze, and wondered if the two of them were an item. The thought annoyed me more than it should. "Are you sure?"

"We're just going to have a drink and talk." Belial's eyes slowly slid to mine. "Isn't that right?"

I held up my cuffs and muttered, "Not much else I can do."

Yumi just shrugged and set down the glasses. "Fine, but let me know if there's any trouble and I'll come right back." She shot me a look of warning and then tossed down her towel. She obviously felt protective of Belial in some way, and the wolf inside me wanted to snap my teeth at her for some odd reason. Luckily she stalked away before I could act on the irrational urge. I had zero reason to feel jealous of her. Nope, none at all.

"What do you want to drink?" Belial asked, shaking me out of my thoughts. Was he really going to pour me a drink like we hadn't been at each other's throats less than an hour ago? What game was he playing? Was he going to poison me? I didn't trust him at all. He had no reason to trust me either, or share a drink with me in his bar like we were old friends catching up after several years apart.

"I'll take whatever you're having," I said, unable to focus enough to actually choose a drink. Belial stepped behind the bar, rolling up his black sleeves and revealing dark tattoos all along his forearms. I watched his chiseled face as he poured us two drinks, just some whiskey on the rocks. I couldn't figure him out at all. What was his deal? Did he really want us to work together?

Was he as disturbed by the disappearances as much as I was, or was he the ultimate villain behind everything? It annoyed me beyond measure that I couldn't trust my instincts on this, and all I could do was watch him closely and try to stay alive.

Once he'd poured us both some whiskey, he leaned against the bar and rested his heavy gaze on me again. "Tell me what you know about the missing shifters."

"I thought you knew everything that happened in your city." I carefully picked up my glass and eyed it, wondering if it was safe.

His broad shoulders moved in a lazy shrug. "I know a lot, but I'm not a shifter. Maybe you know something I don't."

I took a sip of my drink as a test, before telling him anything. I didn't immediately fall to the ground, frothing at the mouth, so there was that at least. I set it down carefully on a coaster, still eyeing it like I was waiting for it to grow legs and walk away. But when the smart burn of the whiskey slid down my throat and I didn't keel over, I decided he truly wasn't going to kill me. At least not now.

I rested my elbows on the bar and met Belial's steady gaze. "Over the last year, at least thirty shifters have gone missing, and all different kinds too. Some just vanished without a trace, but a few of them were last seen in or near New Orleans."

"I had no idea it was that many." He took a long swig of whiskey and then set his own glass down next to mine.

"We've been trying to keep this hidden for as long as we could, but then we learned that some imps have gone missing around here too."

Belial rubbed the stubble on his chin. "I have noticed an

increase in imps attacking humans too over the last few months."

"And no doubt you decided to deal with them with your own vigilante justice," I said dryly.

He gave me an evil grin. "I do what I must to protect my city."

"Uh huh." I shook my head, glaring down at my drink. A drop of condensation traced its way down the side of it and landed on the coaster.

"Archdemon Bastet wanted to investigate. She's the current leader of the shifters, now that my father is dead," I added, just in case Belial was completely out of touch with the world. "She called a meeting between shifters and imps, and Archdemon Loki, who leads the imps, decided that my brothers should be the ones to go to New Orleans to investigate."

Belial leaned forward a bit. "Is there any particular reason he suggested them for the job?"

"Loki thought that if they took care of this problem, it might help the image of the wolf shifters. We're trying to get back into good graces with Bastet and the other shifters after Fenrir's uprising against Lucifer. You know, the one you were involved in?"

"Oh, right, that," Belial said, sounding amused.

I gritted my teeth. How could he be so flippant about the thing that had caused my father's death and the total disgrace of the wolf shifter demons?

"Why would Loki help you?" he asked a moment later, before I could snap something at him. "He's a notorious trickster who cares for no one but himself. It could be a trick."

"It's not a trick," I said through my clenched jaw. "Loki is my grandfather. He's just looking out for us after you killed our father. His *son*."

Belial leaned back but didn't look convinced. Yes, Loki was known for tricking people, even those who thought they were close to him. But he wouldn't do it to family. "Go on," Belial said, motioning for me to continue.

"Skoll and Hati came to New Orleans to investigate two weeks ago. They told me they'd found something, but when I tried to reach out to them a couple of days later, there was no answer. They'd disappeared off the face of the earth, and no one has seen or heard from them since."

My fingers tightened around the whiskey glass, as I remembered the utter terror I'd felt when I couldn't reach them anymore. I'd packed up and flown down here as soon as I could, taking on the investigation myself. But when I'd gotten here, all I'd found was a cold trail, and rumors of the Grim Reaper of New Orleans that was enacting vigilante vengeance around the city. The Grim Reaper...who turned out to be Belial—my father's murderer.

I took another sip of whiskey and made my voice calm again as I looked up at Belial. "When I came to investigate, the only person I found killing shifters was you. No trace of my brothers, or any other leads. Their trail simply went cold."

Belial refilled his whiskey glass as he considered my words. "I have no idea what happened to your brothers, but

I have noticed something odd in the city recently. I've noticed the shifters here have been attacking humans more often than ever before, and when I try to stop them, they're often filled with an almost mindless, animal rage, like they can't control their wrath."

"That's odd," I said, frowning. Shifters always had a problem with rage, of course. We were the demons of wrath, although we could feed on any strong passionate emotion. Anger was just the easiest one to find and provoke.

"The people in New Orleans also seem more violent and angry lately," Belial said. "There's been a major uptick in violent crimes committed every day. The news channels are all telling people to be home before dark just to be safe." He let out a frustrated breath. "I'm doing the best that I can to protect the city, but I can't be everywhere at once. It's getting out of hand, and I'd just like to find the source."

You and me both, I thought, looking him over. He seemed genuinely upset, but he could be a very good actor. I still didn't trust him.

"Do you have any leads at all?" he asked. "You mentioned that your brothers said they found something that could possibly help."

"They never got to share the information with me," I said, shaking my head. "I'm staying at Hotel Immortelle like my brothers were, but I didn't find any information there on what happened to them. It's like they just vanished."

"Hmm." Belial downed the rest of his whiskey in one gulp and then considered me again. "I suggest we get some rest and then start searching. I'm sure you're exhausted after stalking me all night and trying to kill me."

"Does this mean I'll be going back to that wonderful dungeon you have in the basement?" I glared at him. "Are you going to chain me up again?"

"Not if you control yourself." Belial turned a lazy grin on me. "Unless you're into that sort of thing?"

The sultry purr in his voice sent an unwanted rush of desire through me. "With you? No way in hell."

He chuckled low in his throat, like he knew I was lying, as he gathered our glasses and put them in the sink. "Fine, no chains, but you'll stay with me tonight so I can keep an eye on you."

"Lucky me," I muttered. I could already tell this was going to be a long night.

6

EIRA

B elial led me back out the way we'd come and up the stairs again, to a heavy metal door protected by an electronic lock. I watched as Belial unlocked it with a code and then ushered me inside, to what I assumed must be his living room. It was the epitome of masculinity, with exposed brick walls, dark wood framing, and a leather couch that looked both impressive and comfortable. A huge TV sat on one end, while shelves crammed full of books, both new and old, lined the opposite wall. Big windows looked out over the French Quarter, along with a balcony draped in thick, dark curtains. I spotted an open kitchen with dark granite counters and stainless steel appliances, along with a dark metal dining table, and a hallway leading off to more doors, presumably bedrooms. It was all exactly what I'd expect from someone like Belial, except for one thing: the art all along the walls. Dozens of paintings that looked like they came from all different eras, as if he'd stolen each one from a different part of an art museum. I didn't know enough about art to know the artists or even the eras, but I had to admit that the man kept surprising me.

Belial stalked across the room to the hallway, where he grabbed a blanket and a pillow from a cabinet. "You can sleep on the couch."

He shoved both of them at me and I eyed him warily. "You actually expect me to sleep here?"

"Sleep or don't, that's your problem." He loomed over me, his eyes dark and deadly. "Just don't even think about running."

"Or what? You'll chase me down and chain me up again?" I rolled my eyes.

"If you try to run, my horse will stop you."

"Horse?" I asked, looking around. It had to be a metaphor of some sort. "What horse?"

"That one." Belial gestured behind me.

I turned and immediately jumped, because a huge pale gray horse had somehow appeared behind me without making a sound. It was bigger than any horse I'd seen in my life, and had glowing purple eyes. I'd seen a lot of stuff in my time, but I could still be shocked.

"Where the hell did that come from?" I asked, gaping at the horse. Despite it's very equine face, I had the feeling that it was looking at me with disdain, like I was a fly on its back that it could flick away with a single swish of its tail. It probably could. Those purple eyes gave me the creeps.

"Horseman of the Apocalypse, remember?" Belial asked. "It comes with the job."

So maybe he really was Death after all. Shit. No wonder I couldn't kill him. I swallowed hard, as the horse tossed its head in a very haughty manner, and then disappeared again.

"Where did it go?" I asked.

"I don't know," Belial said, shrugging.

"You don't know where your horse goes?" I asked, incredulous.

"Ghost and I respect each other's' privacy," Belial said, like it was the most obvious thing in the world.

Okay then. Maybe Belial was just plain off his rocker. And here I was, stuck with him all night. That did not bode well for me, but at least I'd accepted he wasn't going to kill me just yet. He wouldn't have brought me a pillow and blanket otherwise. I'd much rather be back in my hotel room, but at least I wasn't chained up to a wall in a basement either. At least here I might be able to snoop around and find out more about Belial, including how to defeat him.

"There's not much in the kitchen, but feel free to eat or drink anything you find."

"Let me guess, you're one of those guys who can't cook and orders in every night."

He shot me a hard look. "I'm an excellent cook. But now that I'm an Elder God, I don't need to eat anymore."

My mouth dropped open at that and I fumbled for a good response. "How does someone become an Elder God?"

"It's a long story," he muttered. "Get some rest."

I glanced down at my leather combat gear. "Could I at least go back to my hotel room to grab some clothes?"

"No."

"Fine, I'll just have to sleep in my underwear," I muttered, and started fluffing up the pillow.

"Hang on," he said, his eyes narrowing. He spun on his heel and disappeared down the hallway, then returned a minute later and tossed something at me. "Wear this."

I caught it on reflex, snatching the bundle of fabric out of the air. A black t-shirt, like the one Belial wore.

"Thanks?" I said, making it more of a question than anything else. Belial's eyes flashed again, and he sauntered closer. I held my ground, tilting my chin up. I wasn't going to let him intimidate me, no matter how much taller and stronger he was than me. He didn't stop, getting close enough that if either of us leaned forward just a bit, our chests would brush. He was close enough to kiss.

His mouth opened and closed like he was about to say something, his eyes flashing with annoyance, but then he reached up, touching my hair. He threaded the white strands through his fingers and I sucked in a breath, trying to figure out what he was doing. The action seemed almost involuntary, like he couldn't help himself. For a moment, I was so caught up in it that I couldn't do anything other than sway in and wonder where the hell my night had taken such a weird turn. Then I blinked. *The enemy*, I reminded myself for what seemed like the thousandth time.

"Don't touch me," I said, and then shoved him back as hard as I could.

He was so solid and ridiculously overpowered that even with all of my strength, he hardly swayed. But he stepped back all the same. "Bathroom's down the hall. Get some rest."

What an asshole, I thought, glaring at his retreating form. Once he was gone, I looked around the living room once again. Really, what was I doing? I was staying in this murderer's house like it was no big deal. Unfortunately, he might be my only viable lead, and he might give me clues that could lead me to my brothers. Hopefully I could uncover a way to kill him while I was at it, and finally avenge my father.

Besides, I was trapped here, between the silver cuffs on my wrists and that freaky horse that could show up at any moment out of nowhere to chase me down. Was Belial really Death? That would have been good to know before I'd tried to kill him, but my brothers hadn't mentioned it, and I hadn't heard it from anyone else either. Maybe Lucifer and his people were keeping it on the down low. Not that many people talked about Belial much in the demon world anyway. He'd been an outcast ever since he'd been exiled from Hell hundreds—thousands?—of years ago. All I knew was that he'd been friends with my father...and then he'd killed him.

I looked down at the shirt I was clutching, realizing that I'd clawed the material so much I was distorting the fabric. I smoothed it out, and then lifted it to my nose. I could smell Belial on it, and I was beyond pissed to report that he smelled *amazing.* I debated tossing it aside, but if I was actually going to get some rest, I'd be better off not trying to sleep in my combat gear. With a sigh, and a glance down the hallway to make sure Belial was gone, I began removing my clothes and folding them up. Then I yanked Belial's shirt over my head, inhaling sharply. Unwanted desire rushed through me, making my thighs clench, and I couldn't decide if I wanted to snuggle the shirt even more or tear it off myself. It was surprisingly soft, and large enough to hit me at the top of my thighs.

After a quick trip to the bathroom, I fluffed the pillow once more, and then collapsed onto the couch. I wanted to stay awake and snoop around, or make sure that he wasn't going to murder me, but I was exhausted enough that I couldn't think about doing anything other than lying down.

The moment I closed my eyes, I was sucked directly into sleep. I couldn't have fought it if I'd tried.

I stood in the forest, in the familiar Montana wilds where my pack called home. I looked around, frowning. This wasn't where I'd fallen asleep, was it?

I took a step toward the stream flowing near my feet, where my brothers and I had often splashed as children. When had the direction of the water changed?

The rest of the forest was as dark as night, but I could see the sun in the sky up above. Something was clearly wrong, but I couldn't put my finger on it. I frowned, looking back down at the water. Had it always been that dark? I could have sworn I'd watched fish swim in the clear water many times before.

"*Eira...*"

I looked around, trying to see who was calling my name, but the forest around me was deserted. I turned back to the stream, trying to figure out what was happening and why everything felt so...off.

The voice spoke again, a low, raspy whisper that sounded like something directly from a horror movie. It was clearly female, but not immediately recognizable. "*Eira...*"

"Who's there?" I turned away from the creek, following the general direction of the sound, but no one was there. I couldn't see or smell anyone, but the sound of my name being eerily whispered drifted back to me again.

I spun around as the sound suddenly changed directions, my claws out and ready for a fight, but I was still alone. The eerie weather was really doing a number on me. I dropped my hands, shaking my head and letting out a small huff of laughter at my own paranoia.

A hand closed around my shoulder and I jumped half a foot into the air. A scream escaped my throat, but the sound got choked off when I looked down at the long nails dripping with blood digging into my shoulder.

I wrenched my shoulder away and spun to face the owner, my heart pounding out of my chest. She was dressed in all black, with snakes instead of hair, and a glowing red aura surrounded her. Her face remained indistinguishable, like no matter how hard I looked at her I couldn't quite get her features to stick in my mind.

"Eira," she whispered once again and it sounded like a death rattle from this close up. I shuddered and narrowly

DEATH LORD 43

resisted the urge to brush my shoulder off. I still felt the ghost of her hand on my shoulder. "You have much anger in you."

"No shit," I muttered, although I was feeling a lot more fear than anger at the moment.

"We can help you channel it," another raspy voice said, as a second woman stepped beside the first one. She looked identical to the other woman, except with a green aura around her. "We know you seek vengeance. We can help you find it."

"How?" I looked between the two of them, wondering who they were, and how they possibly thought they could help me.

"Come to us," the first woman hissed, holding her hand out in a beckoning motion.

"We have what you need," the other one said.

She pointed to something behind me, and when I turned around, the world whooshed and I had the distinct feeling of falling forward. I gasped, trying to get my footing, but it didn't seem to matter. The next moment everything coalesced into something solid once again, and I came to a stumbling halt. I gritted my teeth, closing my eyes and trying to stop my head from spinning.

When I opened my eyes again, I drew in a sharp breath. If I knew the clearing by the stream like the back of my hand, this was the exact opposite. I'd never been here before, and I'd certainly remember it. A huge roller coaster stretched above my head, the metal twisting and turning, but it only took a glance for me to realize it was abandoned. Vines grew on the skeletal structure, the metal was rusted in many places, and *the entire concrete base was covered in graffiti art, layered over like people had been coming here for years to mark their spot.*

I started walking toward an old arcade, with broken machines and more graffiti. No one was around and torn flags rustled in the wind, while abandoned carnival prizes lay abandoned and faded. The entire place gave me the creeps, and I wondered what had happened here. Where was everyone?

Somehow I was dead center in an abandoned theme park. I'd never seen it before, but it was distinctive enough that I figured I could find it again once I got out of this... whatever this was. I looked back at the roller coaster, trying to seal it in my mind. Remember this, I told myself.

I continued walking until I stumbled upon a large body of water. It faded into the hazy distance, and I couldn't tell whether it was a large pond or an actual lake. I squinted out at the horizon, and then looked at the half-dead grass under my feet at the bank.

Something was moving in the water. I peered down, trying to get a closer look at it, and then the surface erupted. I jumped back with a scream, stumbling on the uneven ground. From the roiling surface, the two women rose like some sort of eldritch creatures coming to suck the life out of me. I let out another scream and took a few more stumbling steps back.

The women reached for me, their limbs moving weirdly, as if they were puppets on strings that were being jerked in an inhuman way. "Come to us," *the one with the red aura hissed as she lunged forward, as if she planned to attack me.*

I turned around to run, trying to get away, but I couldn't move, my feet suddenly rooted to the ground. I opened my mouth to scream again, but it was sealed shut.

The women moved closer, hands outstretched as if they were trying to pull me toward them through sheer force of will. "Find us," the second hissed, curling her fingers over and over, like she was trying to grip onto me but couldn't quite make it.

I looked around wildly, trying to figure out how to get out of this. There was nothing that could help me and no way to escape. I was glued to the spot, and their fingers would reach me at any moment.

Then a new clarity suddenly hit me. This was where I had to come. The women were right. I needed to find them. They would help me.

I belonged with them.

7

BELIAL

My door burst open. I sat straight up in bed, instantly on high alert. Who would break into my house at night—

Oh, right.

Eira came running into my room, dressed in nothing but the shirt I'd loaned her. I hardly had time to think about her being in my room before my eyes dropped to her legs. The shirt barely covered the tops of her thighs, and I found my cock hardening at the sight.

I'd already been awake when she'd busted through my door, since I didn't need to sleep anymore. I did still try to rest, more out of habit than anything, but one of the perks of being an Elder God was that I didn't need food, sleep, or water anymore. No, instead I had an insatiable thirst to steal souls, although it had been much weaker ever since meeting her, like her mere presence nearby calmed the urge. I'd been tempted to stare at her while she slept, trying to figure out what made her different, but I'd forced myself to stay in my room instead.

Eira's eyes dropped to my naked chest, her mouth opening slowly. At first, she seemed as caught up in the lust as I was, but then she shook her head violently and then looked back up at my face. Still, words seemed to fail her.

"Have you come to try to kill me again?" I asked, stretching my arms behind my head in a way that I knew would draw her attention. "Or are you in my bedroom for something else?"

Her eyes widened at my words, and her nostrils flared a little as her eyes traced the tattoos on my arms and the muscles in my chest, before going lower, to where the sheet had pooled around my hips. I always slept in the nude. Who knew it would be useful to put a mouthy shifter in her place?

"No way in hell," Eira finally spat.

"I can take you to Hell if you'd prefer, though I assure you my bed is more comfortable."

Eira huffed out an annoyed breath. "Could you shut up for two seconds? I had a...dream."

"What kind of dream?" I asked, arching an eyebrow.

"Not that kind." She rubbed her hands over her arms as if they were cold. "There were these two women..." She paused and then shook her head. "I don't know if *women* is a good descriptor. They had these long claws and hair made out of snakes. They told me to find them."

A chill ran down my spine at her description. I had a feeling I knew who she'd been dreaming about, though I hoped I was wrong. I slid out of bed, my thoughts moving quickly as I planned what to do next, but then Eira gasped and turned around. *Oh, right. Naked.*

"Can you at least give me a warning next time?" she growled. "And put some damn clothes on!"

"You're in my bedroom," I reminded her. "What, did you like what you saw a little too much?"

"In your dreams," Eira snapped.

I pulled on some loose sweatpants so Eira could focus, because I was sure she wouldn't be able to if I stayed naked. No matter how much fun it was to tease her, I needed to figure out if this dream that had freaked her out so much was actually anything to be worried about.

"I might know who you saw," I said. "The Furies. Did you happen to see a third one?"

Eira shook her head, frowning. "No, just the two."

"That's odd. They always come in a group of three. Never less." I grabbed a t-shirt and pulled it on. "Are you sure that's what you saw? Could it have been something else? Describe them to me again."

Eira looked annoyed, her hands going to her hips. "Yes, that's what I saw. They had snakes for hair, nails dripping with blood, and auras of color around them—one green and one red. I couldn't see their faces."

"That's how they looked in the old days when they walked the Earth." I ran a hand along my jaw, as I took in this new complication. "They're Elder Gods, and should be trapped in Void like most of the others. They have the ability to send images and dreams to people, even across great distances, but they shouldn't be able to do that unless they were somehow here in this realm."

"The Furies?" Eira asked.

"Yes, goddesses of anger, jealousy, and vengeance. They caused a lot of havoc in ancient times, before they were sealed away with the rest of the Elder Gods. But no one's heard anything about them in centuries, as far as I know."

"Well, that's what I saw." She bit her lip, her eyes distant. "I feel this odd compulsion to go to them, like I can't help myself, even now. I'm fighting it, but it's like someone's attached a string in my stomach and is pulling on it."

Shit. This was really not good. My parents and I were supposed to be the only Elder Gods on Earth right now, but if the Furies were somehow getting into people's heads, they had to be close "I wonder if they got the other shifters that way."

"You think they're the ones who are getting the shifters? I guess that would make sense." She tapped her finger on her lips as she thought, and I found myself looking at them again, wondering what they tasted like.

"Where were you in the dream?" I asked, trying to tear my own thoughts away from her allure.

"There was this old roller coaster that looked like it hadn't been used in years. It was in a theme park, and the whole thing was abandoned. There was a big pond or lake at the edge of it, and the Furies rose out of that."

I nodded slowly. "Sounds like Jazzland. It was an amusement park on the edge of New Orleans that was abandoned after it was destroyed by Hurricane Katrina."

"Sounds creepy," Eira said, shuddering.

"Very. It's rumored to be haunted, but then again, what isn't haunted in New Orleans?"

Eira shrugged at that and followed me from my bedroom to the living room. She didn't seem to be interested in going back to sleep, so I headed for the kitchen and started the coffee maker. Through the windows, the horizon was starting to lighten, and the sun would be coming up soon.

Eira sat at the island counter while the coffee began brewing. I stood over the sink and stared out the window at the city as it woke up, though it would still be hours before it really got moving. I'd never even considered that another Elder God might be loose, let alone *two*. Fucking hell.

My guest didn't speak either, her eyes staring off into space as though she was reliving the horrors of the dream. A fierce protective urge settled over me at the thought of the Furies targeting her, and I found myself pulling out some old cereal from my cupboard and pouring it into a bowl for her. I didn't have much food in my place anymore, but she needed to eat something. I added some milk, which I kept for my coffee, and then slid it in front of her.

"What's this?" she asked, blinking at it.

"Breakfast." I poured her a cup of coffee next. "How do you like your coffee? Black like your heart?"

She scowled at me, but at least the vacant look in her eyes was gone. "With lots of sugar and milk, actually."

"Ah, you're one of those types who likes coffee that doesn't taste like coffee."

"Exactly," she said, as she poured a ridiculous amount of

stuff into her mug. "Why would the Furies be luring shifters to them?"

"I don't know, but it can't be good. The Furies are incredibly dangerous." I took a swig of coffee before continuing. "Like all Elder Gods, they embody primordial elements of the universe and can't be completely destroyed. They were originally good, seeking to take out the evil of the world, but they got bloodthirsty and decided that *all* humans needed to be punished."

Eira snorted as she stirred her cereal. "Sounds a lot like what you're doing."

I leaned forward on the counter, my eyes narrowing at her. "I only kill those who have hurt others. People who need to be stopped, who the police can't or won't deal with."

Eira shrugged. "You're still a murderer. No matter how you try to justify it."

"You were going to murder me too, where you not?"

"That's different," she said. "I was stopping you from killing someone else."

"Exactly the same thing I was doing," I muttered, but I knew she wouldn't listen. She was too damn stubborn and had already created this narrative in her head where I was the bad guy. Okay, fine, I'd killed her father, but he'd needed to be stopped before he destroyed the whole freaking world.

"Go get dressed," I said curtly as I set my mug in the sink. "We're going to Jazzland to figure out why you're dreaming about it."

"We're going now?" Eira asked as she slid off the stool. I carefully didn't look at her exposed legs. I didn't need to tempt myself any more than I already was. It was clear that we weren't going to be anything more than reluctant allies, but that didn't seem to matter to my dick.

"Why wait?" I asked with a shrug.

"Fine with me," she said, rubbing at her stomach with a frown. "The need to go there is getting stronger every minute."

"Even more reason to go sooner than later. You can have the first shower."

She headed for the bathroom, and I watched the door long after she had disappeared behind it. The sound of the shower turned on and desire raged inside of me, as unquenchable as my thirst for death. I wanted to follow her into the bathroom, to see what would happen if I climbed in with her and began soaping that smooth skin or slid my fingers between those lush thighs.

Instead, I stomped back into my room and slammed the door, then grabbed my cock in my pants and jerked it hard, trying to relieve the pressure there. I pictured Eira soaping herself, running her hands along her body, as my hand slid along my cock, faster and faster. Then I imagined myself bending her over and fucking her from behind as the water sprayed onto us, while she cried my name and begged for more. The thought had me coming hard into my hand, but when I was done, I only wanted more. Only she could truly sate me.

Fuck. This non-stop pull toward Eira was becoming a real problem. Even worse, I had a feeling I knew what it was. I'd been trying to deny it ever since we met, but the urge to mate was only growing stronger by the minute. Soon I feared it would become overwhelming, and we'd be unable to stop what was coming next.

I knew this, because I'd lived through it once before—and this time it felt even stronger. Was it possible to have a second fated mate?

And how could I have one at all, when I had no soul?

8

EIRA

The urge to find the Furies, if that's truly who they were, grew with every moment that passed. By the time I followed Belial outside to his garage, the incessant pull was almost painful, like I was being dragged forward by my ankles, and only sheer willpower stopped me from dropping everything and taking off in a run. Well, maybe sheer willpower plus the other strange attraction I was feeling toward Belial. My pull toward him was equally strong, and at times it felt like I was going to be torn apart between the two conflicting forces.

He swung the keys around his finger as he circled a black Ducati motorcycle in the middle of his garage. He climbed on the bike with ease, and I hated how my eyes followed him, devouring his every movement. Seeing him naked earlier had set something off in me like a ticking time bomb of lust, and now I couldn't stop drooling over the asshole, even though I definitely was not going to fuck him. Even if he was the hottest guy I'd ever seen.

"Get on," he said, once he was seated on the bike.

"You have wings and a spectral horse, yet you ride a motorcycle?" I asked, mostly to hide my apprehension at climbing onto the bike behind him. There was not much room there, which meant I would be pressed along that big, hard body for the entire journey. I wanted it and dreaded it all at once.

"You can turn into a wolf, but you don't run around the city like that, do you?" Belial shot back. "I've been alive for thousands of years on Earth because I know how to blend in with humans."

"Walking around in a hooded cape at night is not exactly 'blending in,'" I said.

He snorted at that, but eyed me closely. "How old are you, anyway?"

"I just turned forty," I said, standing a little taller. Among immortal demons, age was measured in centuries, not decades, but I wasn't ashamed of my youth.

Belial let out a sharp laugh. "You're not even a century old. Practically still a child."

"You didn't think I was a child when you almost kissed me last night, old man," I snapped.

"And you definitely didn't think I was an old man when you ogled my naked body this morning. Now hurry up and get on the bike already."

I huffed and climbed onto the bike behind him. He wore

a t-shirt that clung to his muscular chest—which, yes, I'd seen in *great* detail this morning—and showed off the tattoos that ran all along his arms. I tried not to touch him, but then the bike lurched forward and I found myself clinging to Belial to stay on it as we zoomed out of the garage and onto the street. The second my hands wrapped around those strong arms I felt that annoying spark between us, which only made me want to press my entire body against his. And that spot of his neck in my face was just begging for me to lean forward and set my mouth there.

I closed my eyes and breathed in deeply, trying to get myself under control as we drove out of the French Quarter and onto the highway. Between Belial and the Furies, I was losing my damn mind. Luckily, the ride was shorter than I thought it would be, and before I knew it, Belial was killing the engine on his bike. We were just off the side of a deserted road with dense plants on either side of us, and he gestured for me to hop off, then hid the bike in some shrubbery.

"Is this the place?" I asked, as my gut tried to tug me forward. *Keep going, almost there,* it seemed to whisper deep inside me.

Belial nodded. "We'll walk the rest of the way. Stay alert in case we're attacked."

"You know what would help with that?" I asked as we started moving through the trees and bushes. "If you took these cuffs off me so I could shift or use magic."

Belial kept charging through the foliage without looking back. "Not going to happen."

"I'm not going to run, if that's what you're worried about. I'm here to find out what happened to my brothers and the other shifters. I need answers."

"I'm less worried about you running and more about you trying to kill me again."

I rolled my eyes. "You're really hung up on that, aren't you? Especially for a guy who supposedly can't be killed."

"It's more of an annoyance than a real problem," Belial growled. "Thanks to you, that shifter got away last night. He'll probably be out there tonight trying to kill someone else. Which means I'll have to be out there too to make sure he doesn't. And if he does kill some innocent person? That's on you."

"Once again, the only person I saw trying to commit murder was you." I picked at the silver cuffs on my wrists, wishing I could get them off. "But if you're so worried, I'll help you watch over your city tonight. As long as you remove the cuffs, that is."

"Nope."

I shrugged. "Well, I had to try."

"Shut up and stay close," he said, as we came to the edge of the bushes.

In front of us was a faded, rusty sign that said, "Six Flags New Orleans" and below it, "Closed For Storm," except the first O was missing. We continued forward and climbed over a fence, while the Louisiana heat washed over me. With my shifter and Winter fae blood, I always preferred a cool, dark night over a sunny day, but if we did run into a group of demons, they'd be weaker at this time. Most imps and shifters would usually be sleeping now. That could give us an advantage.

Up ahead, rusted roller coasters loomed over the entire abandoned amusement park, which was somehow creepier in real life than it had been in my dream. We passed empty buildings that once sold food and tourist gifts, but were now covered in graffiti, their windows broken, their doors hanging off the hinges. You could almost hear the echoes of children playing and laughing along the cracked cement, a reminder that a place like this should never be so empty and lifeless. No wonder people thought it was haunted.

I lifted my nose to the air, hoping to catch the scent of another living being in this park with my shifter senses, but then I remembered the damn cuffs that blocked my magic. Damn Belial. I would get these cuffs off somehow.

The rest of the park was just as desolate, although nature had crept in and was slowly taking over the area. Debris littered the area, weeds and plants had grown up over everything, and I jumped at the sight of an actual alligator sitting beside the remains of a carousel. I nudged Belial but he just shrugged like he saw alligators all the time, but *he* still had his powers. I was basically a defenseless human right now.

Join us, a voice whispered in my ear. I whipped around, looking to see if anyone was there, but saw no one but Belial. "Did you hear that?"

"Hear what?" Belial asked, giving me an odd look.

I opened my mouth to tell him, but before I could, a

rustling sound in the bushes caught our attention. Someone was out there, moving toward us. No—a lot of someones, and they were coming from every direction, forming a circle around us. My hands formed into fists, and I wished again that I had my magic or at least a weapon of some sort. Belial just stood beside me, taking it all in, his face hard and his eyes completely fearless.

Even without my wolf senses I could tell most of these people were shifters from the way they moved, although I guessed a few of them were imps too. They drew closer, surrounding us completely, cutting off every escape route. There was no chance to turn and head back to the entrance, and short of Belial breaking out his wings and flying us out, we were trapped.

"I'm pretty sure we just walked into an ambush," I muttered.

Before either of us could discuss what we were going to do to get the hell out of here, two giant wolves prowled forward. One was black with red eyes, while the other was white with blue eyes, but otherwise they were identical. As they stepped through the brush, their claws burned it and turned it to ash.

My heart leaped at the sight of my brothers, completely unharmed, and I rushed forward. "Skoll! Hati!"

Belial grabbed my arm and held me back with his supernatural strength. I glared at him and jerked at my arm, but he didn't let me go.

"They're my brothers, you big dumb oaf!" I turned back

to them. "I'm so glad to see you guys. You have no idea how worried I've been. Why haven't you returned my calls or anything?"

Neither one of them answered, and both of my brothers stared at me like they had no idea who I was. When I stepped toward them again, they growled low in their throats.

Belial shoved me behind him, protecting me with his body. Which was totally unnecessary, because my older brothers would never hurt me. Would they?

"What are you doing here?" I asked them, stepping out from behind Belial.

"We're working with the Furies now," Skoll said, his wolf voice like a low growl. His red eyes blazed with inner fire as he stared us down like he was about to lunge.

Hati's claws scraped at the ground, turning the grass to ash. "You should join us too."

I frowned at my brothers, wondering why they were acting this way. Sure, they were both assholes, but this was different. This was wrong.

"Where are the Furies?" Belial asked.

"You..." Skoll said with a snarl. "We've been waiting for a chance to get you alone."

"Thanks for bringing him to us, Eira," Hati added. "Now we will tear him apart."

I held up a hand. "Yeah, I already tried that and it didn't go so well. The bastard's basically unkillable. But that's not why I'm here, anyway."

Hati crept closer, teeth bared. "Maybe you just weren't up to the task."

"Now it's our turn," Skoll said at his side. "Time to die."

Shadows gathered around Belial as he faced them down. "Try it, and we'll see who ends up dead."

I stepped in front of Belial this time, my pulse racing. I couldn't let my brothers attack—they had no idea how dangerous Belial was, and they'd probably both end up dead. But how would I stop them? They looked like they were about to tear through me to get to Belial.

"Now, now, let's not fight with our guests," a woman's voice said from behind us.

Hati and Skoll stopped immediately at the sound, lowering their heads in submission, though they continued to glare at us with obvious hatred. I gaped at the sight of them, then turned toward the voice.

Two hooded figures made their way through the ranks of shifters and imps, who parted around them without having to be told. I didn't have to see the women's faces to know that these were the Furies. My hackles went up and a chill ran across my skin as both of them stopped in front of us and threw their hoods back. They looked completely different from the women from my dream—the hair snakes and bloody claws were gone, for one thing—but they still radiated the same power.

"Welcome," one of the women said. She was tall and thin, with short black hair, tanned skin, and features that were more stern than pretty. "We knew you would come."

"You sent me the dream, didn't you?" I asked.

"Yes, and we're so pleased you brought Death with you," the other woman replied. Unlike her sister—who she looked nothing like—she was one of the most beautiful women I'd ever seen, with long, shiny chestnut hair and legs that seemed to go on for miles, along with a slitted dress to show them off. "We've been wondering when he would visit us."

"I see you've found yourselves some new bodies to possess," Belial drawled. "Which ones are you?"

"I am Anger, though you may call me Alecto," the black-haired one said, somehow making it sound like a threat. She gestured toward her sister. "And this is Jealousy, who some call Megaera."

"How did you get to Earth?" Belial asked.

"A portal opened in Void, and we felt Death calling," Megaera said.

Belial crossed his arms. "I didn't call you."

"Not you. The previous Death." Alecto's eyes narrowed, as if this was a sore spot. "We came through, but the portal closed too quickly for our third sister to make it. Now we must bring her to Earth, so we can continue our goal of punishing wicked humans."

"We served the previous Death," Megaera said, batting her eyelashes at Belial. "We would be willing to work with you too. We can give you *whatever* you need."

Jealousy rose up in me at the way she looked at Belial, and then I realized that was what she wanted. I suspected they both inspired and fed on the emotions they embodied.

To my relief, Belial didn't seem to care one bit about her offer, because he let out a sharp laugh. "How about you serve me by going back to Void? You don't belong on Earth, and there's only room for one Elder God in this city."

Alecto's eyes suddenly glowed red as she looked at him with pure fury. Apparently Belial's ability to piss off anything with a heartbeat extended to the Furies too. "If you won't work with us, then stay out of our way." The 'or else' was implied.

"Why are you gathering shifters and imps here?" I asked, as Belial stared them down.

Megaera turned her gaze on me and smiled in a way that felt almost predatory. "Those who are attuned to wrath and jealousy are simply drawn to us. You've felt it yourself, haven't you?"

"Let them go," Belial said in a low, dangerous voice. "These people are not yours to control."

Megaera laughed. "What if they don't want to leave?"

My brothers moved beside the two women, brushing up against them in a protective and almost loving way. They snarled at us, making it clear they would defend the Furies if we tried to attack them. The other people all around us seemed to step forward too, reminding us we were surrounded and outnumbered. Belial squared his shoulders and gathered more shadows around him, obviously ready to fight. But if we attacked, a lot of lives would be lost, and I wasn't sure who would come out the victor.

I touched Belial's arm to get his attention. "We should go."

He jerked his gaze to the spot where I was touching him, and then his eyes lifted to meet mine. His brow furrowed, like he was torn on what to do, but then he nodded. He shot the Furies a sharp look. "This isn't over."

I sighed and released him, relieved that he wasn't going to attack. We started to leave, but then a shiver ran down my spine.

Stay, a voice said in my head. *Join us.*

Both Furies stared at me intently, along with my brothers. I shook my head and looked away, trying to ignore the voices filling my head.

You have so much wrath in your heart. Don't you want vengeance?

Only we can give you what you want.

Shut up, I shot back, covering my ears even though I knew it wouldn't help. Belial gave me a questioning look.

Our sister is the Elder God of vengeance.

She can help you defeat Belial.

All you have to do is help us bring her to Earth...

I stopped dead in my tracks as their voices filled my head and took hold of me. Vengeance. Yes. I wanted that with such a deep pull that I actually felt myself take a couple of steps toward them. I would finally get closure for my father's death and extract my revenge on Belial. Rage surged inside me at the thought of him, along with jealousy of his powers. Why should he be alive, when my father wasn't? He had to die to pay for his sins. All it would take was—

"Eira, what is it?" Belial asked, gripping my arms tight.

His voice and his touch shook me out of the Furies' trance. I gaped at him as my head cleared and the rage and jealousy died down. Shit, that had been intense. Still, I couldn't deny that their offer wasn't tempting...

"Nothing," I said, taking a deep breath to steady myself. I jerked my eyes away from the Furies and focused on Belial instead. "Let's get out of here."

9

EIRA

I walked into Belial's bar in a daze, and it wasn't until we were seated at the counter that I realized we hadn't gone back to his apartment. I glanced around, surprised Belial wasn't worried about people seeing me in cuffs, but the place was empty except for us.

"Don't worry, it's not open yet," Belial said, like he could read my mind. "I thought you could use a drink, along with some food."

I nodded, still shaken by what we'd uncovered at the amusement park. While it was a relief to know my brothers and all those other missing shifters were alive, it was just as disturbing to see they'd fallen under the Furies' spell and become completely different people. If I'd stayed, would I have ended up like them too?

Belial poured me a beer, and then disappeared into another room behind the bar. I stared at my drink, going over everything that had happened, searching for more clues or a reason as to why the Furies were doing this. Eventually, Belial came back with a burger and fries, and set it down in front of me. The smell of hot feed made me perk up a little.

"Where did you get this?" I asked.

"The cooks are already here," Belial replied. "It's not poisoned, I promise. You look like you're about two minutes away from passing out. Eat."

He wasn't wrong. I ducked my head and dug into the surprisingly delicious food, while he watched me like he was studying me again.

"You really don't eat at all?" I asked.

He plucked a fry off my plate and tossed it in his mouth. "I can eat. I just don't need to."

I pulled my plate away from him. "Hey, get your own damn fries."

He smirked and reached for another one. "You're in my bar, so I think technically they're my fries."

I slapped at his hand. "Nope, you gave them to me. Mine now."

The smirk turned into an amused grin. "Would it make you feel better if I got my own food?"

"Much."

"Fine." He stomped into the back again, leaving me alone for a few minutes. Unfortunately, that left me alone again with my thoughts.

I didn't trust the Furies at all. Why were they luring shifters there? Did it have something to do with bringing their missing third sister to Earth? I shuddered as I remembered how it had felt to be under their compulsion, with their words rattling around my head. I needed to get my brothers away from them before they ended up hurt...or worse.

But a tiny voice inside me was curious about their offer too. I still wanted vengeance for my father, but I'd found no way to defeat Belial so far. If the Furies were telling the truth, they could help me defeat him. Which I still wanted. Right?

I wasn't so sure anymore. The last twenty-four hours had thrown everything in my world upside down. I'd come to New Orleans with the image of a clear-cut killer in my head, and I was ready to make him pay. But Belial had turned out to be different than I'd expected, and now I didn't know what to think. Yes, he was a total dick, and if he didn't take these cuffs off my wrist soon I was going to scream, but I didn't believe he was a cold-blooded murderer anymore. He seemed to really care about protecting New Orleans and finding out what was happening with the missing people, plus he'd protected me at the amusement park. Not to mention, there was that intense pull I felt toward him, though I was trying to ignore that as much as I possibly could.

Belial returned with his own burger and fries, but he remained standing behind the bar as he ate them. Did he want to keep some distance between us? Or was he standing over me to remind me he was the boss here?

I sighed as I finished off the last of my fries. "What are we going to do about the Furies?"

"We?" Belial asked, arching an eyebrow. "Are we on the same side now?"

"No, but we have a common enemy."

"Glad to know you feel that way. I was worried you might go over to their side, like the other shifters did."

"I almost did, until you shook me out of it," I admitted. "The Furies were inside my head, trying to convince me to join them. But more than that, there was this compulsion that I couldn't resist, like a voice inside me telling me to do whatever they said. By the time you stopped me, I was about two steps away from joining their little cult."

Belial stroked the dark stubble on his chin. "That must be how they got the other demons to fall under their sway. Shifters feed on wrath, while imps feed on envy, which Alecto and Megaera can create and control. If they used that in conjunction with their ability to get into people's heads, it's possible they could compel the demons to join them. But since you're part fae, perhaps you're more able to resist them."

"Maybe," I said, though I wasn't sure how good I'd been at resisting them. I had been closer to giving up and letting them have me than I'd like to admit, and I wasn't sure if I'd be able to stop them if they tried again. "They've turned my brothers into loyal guard dogs. How can we break their control?"

"I'm still figuring that out." He took a long sip of his beer as he considered. "Although sending them back to Void would do it."

"What exactly is this Void place?" I asked.

"An alternate realm where the Elder Gods are trapped. That's all anyone really knows. It's been sealed off for thousands of years."

"If it's sealed off, how are the Furies going to bring their sister over?"

"I wish I knew. They don't have a key to Void, or they would have done it already, but there are always other ways to open portals. It just depends on how much they know, and how far they're willing to go."

"But there must be a way to defeat them," I said. *And you*, I mentally added.

"They're Elder Gods, like me, so they can't be killed," he said. "We could kill the bodies they're possessing, but just like you can't remove all anger or jealousy from the world, we can't destroy them either. We need to either contain them in a specially crafted tomb made by the fae, or use a Void key to open a portal to send them back."

"And we don't have either one of those," I said with a groan.

"Nope."

Getting a tomb made by the fae would take too long, I suspected. If they agreed to help us at all. You never knew with the fae. "How do we get a Void key then?"

Belial smirked again, his eyes flashing with dark humor. "Why, so you can use it on me next?"

I hid my smile with my drink. "Well, now that you've given me the idea…"

He shook his head, but didn't seem especially worried. "My father had one, and together we were able to send Pestilence back to Void, but apparently we unknowingly let two Furies in at the same time. But the Void key was destroyed, and I'm not sure where to get another."

I tapped my fingers on the bar as I pondered our next move. "I could ask Loki. If there's anyone who knows how to find some rare artifact, it's probably him."

"Loki?" Belial practically spat the name. "Could we really trust anything the trickster tells us?"

"Do you have any better ideas?" I tilted my head, staring him down. "Ask your parents, maybe?"

He grimaced at that. "No way. Besides, they're in Hell right now, and I don't have a key to go *there* either."

"Sounds like Loki is our best option then." I extended my hand. "Give me back my phone and I'll text him now."

Belial scowled at me, but he reached in his pocket and got out my phone, then slid it along the bar. I grabbed it and immediately saw a message from my friend Mirabella asking me if I was okay. She was half-fae and half-demon like me, and together we'd worked as messengers between the two sides, going back and forth between Earth and Faerie. I'd given up the job once my father started his rebellion against Lucifer, but I'd remained friends with Mirabella through it all. I shot her off a quick reply, saying I was fine and I'd catch up with her soon, then sent another message to Loki, asking if I could talk to him, noting that it was urgent. Hopefully he would respond quickly. Loki was the kind of guy who called on you when he felt like it, not the other way around.

"I sent him a message," I said, and then quickly stashed the phone in my pocket before Belial could try to take it away. "Hopefully he responds soon. He'll likely want to meet in person."

Belial rested his hands on the bar on either side of me, towering over me. "If you're going to see him, I'm coming with you."

"Only if you play nice. He won't help us if you're rude."

"I'm always nice."

"We both know that's not true." I held up my cuffs. "If you were, you'd take these off and let me go back to my hotel."

"No, I think it's best I keep an eye on you." He cocked his head. "But I suppose we could get your things from the hotel."

"So you plan to keep me a prisoner for a while?" I asked, holding up my hands. The silver cuffs winked in the light, and his eyes fell to them.

"For now, yes. Show me you can be trusted, and maybe that will change."

"How exactly am I supposed to do that?" I asked, blowing out a breath in frustration.

He caught my wrists in his hands. "Stop fighting me and we'll find out."

At his touch, electricity seemed to zip along my skin, and my heart skipped a beat. His thumbs slowly rubbed my skin along the edge of the cuffs as he stared into my eyes, and within them I saw a hunger there that made my breath catch.

"I'm not fighting you," I said, my voice little more than a whisper. I bit my lip, and his gaze flickered to the motion, and then came back up to my eyes. The need in his eyes grew stronger, and he pulled me forward by the wrists, making me lean against the bar.

One of his hands came up to slide into my hair, turning my head slightly. His nose brushed along my neck as he breathed me in, and all I could do was melt into his touch, craving more. His breath moved across my skin lightly, traveling up my neck and to my chin and then to my mouth, where I eagerly waited for him to kiss me. Or throw me down on this bar and spread my legs for him.

Then a door banged open, and the spell was broken.

I jumped back, yanking away from Belial as I turned to face the sound. Yumi, the bartender from last night, stood in the doorway, her eyes moving between us. She looked at me suspiciously for a few moments and then headed toward the bar, shaking her head. Belial busied himself with tidying up our empty drinks, his face calm and collected, like we hadn't just been about to kiss...or more.

"Can you handle the bar tonight?" he asked Yumi. "I have something I need to handle."

"Of course." Yumi shot me another long glance, but nodded at Belial. "Be safe."

"It's not me you need to worry about," he said with a grunt as he stepped out from behind the bar.

"Are you so sure about that?" Yumi asked, crossing her arms as she stared at me.

What was her deal? Did she have a thing for Belial? Jealousy surged inside me at the thought, but I pushed it away. I felt her gaze burning holes in my back until we exited the bar.

10

EIRA

This time we took one of Belial's cars, a black Aston
Martin, and headed into the Garden District along
oak-shaded streets. Belial's hands were tight on the steering
wheel the whole time, and a muscle in his jaw ticked in an
almost rhythmic way. I wasn't sure what his problem was,
and told myself I didn't care either.

His bad mood only got worse when we pulled up to the
grand historic mansion with white columns and wrought-
iron balconies. Hotel Immortelle had once been a wealthy
family's home in the 1800s, but now it was a luxury hotel
catering to demons and other supernaturals who visited the
city. It was far more elegant than anywhere my brothers and
I would have stayed on our own, but since we'd been visiting
the city on official demon business, Loki had insisted we stay
there. I couldn't deny the place was gorgeous though, and it
was refreshing to stay at a hotel where they understood the
special needs of demons. They even had lush, private

grounds out back where shifters could roam freely in their animal forms.

A valet took the car and Belial scowled at the man, then looked up at the hotel like he was waiting for it to explode. "Get your things quickly."

"What's your problem?" I asked, as we stepped through the big black doors and into the lobby, which was just as luxurious as the rest of the hotel with an abundance of mirrors and gold gilding. A man by the front desk offered us aperitifs with or without blood (for the vampires, naturally), but we waved him away as we headed for the elevator.

"I've always hated this place."

"Any particular reason?"

"My father owns it," he said grudgingly. "We have some...issues. We've mostly worked them out, but I'd prefer to not hang around the place any more than I have to."

I should have known Lucifer owned the place. As ruler of the demons, he seemed to have his hand in just about everything. It was one reason my father had rebelled against him—too much power in the hands of one immortal ruler was dangerous. Of course, my father had failed and had paid the ultimate price for his crimes.

"Hard to imagine anyone having issues with you, with your glowing personality," I said as we entered the elevator, my voice dripping with sarcasm. "Especially Lucifer, since you tried to overthrow him with my father." I stabbed at the button for the third floor, while smooth jazz music played around us. "You know, before you killed him."

He shook his head. "You have no idea what happened with your father."

When the elevator door opened, I led the way down the hall toward my room, while Belial followed right at my heels. "So tell me what happened. From your point of view."

I swiped my key and the door clicked open. Inside, the room was large enough that we didn't feel cramped in it even with a huge four-posted bed and old-fashioned French furniture. My luggage was open in the corner with a few clothes spilling out of it. I tried not to feel self conscious as I slung a bra in alongside a shirt.

Belial sat in a wingback chair opposite the bed, and flipped on the Tiffany lamp beside him, causing the colored glass to shoot light across his handsome face. "Your father and I were...allies, if not exactly friends. We both wanted to see change come for the demons, and believed that a new ruler would be the best thing for everyone. So we decided to take down Lucifer, once and for all."

"Why?" I asked from the bathroom as I gathered up my toiletries. "He's your father."

"Lucifer had gone unchecked for too long. He was out of touch with what most demons wanted, and wouldn't listen to anyone who disagreed with him. He made rash decisions without consulting anyone, like ending the war with the angels and closing off Hell forever. But he's so damn powerful, no one dared oppose him openly."

"My father said similar things," I said. He'd always tried to keep me out of his rebellion against Lucifer, partly for my safety and partly to keep me more neutral since I worked as a messenger with the fae, but I'd heard him ranting about our ruler for my whole life. I'd never met Lucifer, but I'd been raised to hate him.

"The last person who had tried to oppose Lucifer...was me." Belial gave me a sardonic smirk as he continued. "That was what got me kicked out of Hell all those years ago. For my rebellion, he condemned me to live on Earth."

"The exiled prince," I said with a nod as I finished packing. Everyone in the demon world knew the story of Lucifer's eldest son trying to claim the throne, and being punished for it. It was no wonder Belial had some serious daddy issues. But with a father like Lucifer, who wouldn't?

"Yes, they love to call me that," Belial said, rolling his eyes. "But this time when I decided to overthrow my father, I wanted things to be different. Fenrir and I made a plan, and we got the help of some of the other Archdemons who felt the same way we did about Lucifer. Together we planned to awaken the Four Horsemen of the Apocalypse to defeat Lucifer, since he was too strong for any of us to take down on our own." His face darkened as he stared out the window, his eyes lost in the memory. "But once Pestilence was freed, I realized we'd made a huge mistake."

By now I'd finished packing, and I sat on the edge of the bed, eager to hear his story and finally have some answers. "Why did you change your mind?"

"Pestilence was too damn powerful and he wanted nothing more than to annihilate the entire world. That wasn't what I'd signed up for. Earth has been my home for centuries, and I didn't want it destroyed. I just wanted Lucifer overthrown."

"I mean, they are called the Four Horsemen of the *Apocalypse* for a reason," I said. "What did you think would happen?"

He scowled in response. "I was a fool. I'd been a child when the Four Horsemen were first defeated and entombed, but I'd forgotten how bad things had gotten then. Once Pestilence was freed and began spreading plague across the world, I knew I had to stop him. We freed War and I tried to use him to take down Pestilence, since the best way to defeat an Elder God is with another Elder God. But War needed a body to possess, as all Elder Gods do, and Lucifer sacrificed himself to save me from being possessed." His scowl only deepened at the memory, and he ran a hand through his hair. "My mother then became Famine to take *him* down."

I nodded slowly. "I was there when your mother freed Famine. My father needed me to open the portal to Faerie, where Famine was entombed, and I saw the horrible aftermath once she was set lose. Famine actually tried to possess my body." I shuddered a little at the memory of the Elder God draining my life away from me. "Your mother saved me when she let Famine possess her. Fenrir and I escaped before I saw what happened next though."

"She's impressive, isn't she? She's the reincarnation of Eve and has been many things in her past lives, but I think she's topped them all in her current life." He grinned at the mention of his mother, obviously fond of her. "She found a way to defeat the Elder God when it was inside her—basically resisting the possession while retaining all of the powers of Famine. She managed to save Lucifer, who defeated War and took possession of his own body again too."

"What happened next?" I asked. "How did Death get free?"

Belial's grin fell and darkness clouded his face again. "After all that happened, I couldn't stand against my father anymore. Yes, he'd fallen short as a leader many times, but he was still my father. He'd sacrificed himself to save me. He wasn't perfect, but he and I talked some things out, and he seemed open to changing how he ruled. But Fenrir didn't want to stop."

My muscles tensed, knowing what was coming. I had to know what happened, but I didn't want to hear it either.

"By then, most of our other allies had been killed, but Fenrir teamed up with Pestilence, thinking they would overthrow Lucifer together and then he would crown himself the new king of demons. They released Death, who possessed Fenrir's body, and they kidnapped my baby sister, Aurora, and took her to Hell." His hands clenched the sides of the chair at the memory. "My parents led an army into Hell to rescue her, and this time, I fought alongside them to rescue my sister and stop the Horsemen from destroying the world."

"And my father?" I asked, my voice barely above a whisper.

"By the time we fought, there was very little of him left inside his body. Death was completely in control, and I doubted Fenrir even wanted to fight him off. The only way to stop him was to kill him."

I swallowed, my throat dry, as I learned about this for the first time. My father had said it was too dangerous for me to come with him to Hell to release Death, and most of the shifters who had gone with him had either died or refused to talk about it. I'd learned about my father's death from my brothers, who had been there at the battle in Hell, but they hadn't told me all of this. They'd painted Belial as the villain, and made me crave vengeance for the death of our father, but now I knew the truth was a lot more complicated than I could have imagined. I'd loved my father, but he'd been no saint, and I'd seen him lose more and more of himself in his quest to become the king of demons near the end. Maybe I should have tried harder to stop him too.

Belial's eyes met mine. "I want you to know I took no joy in ending your father's life, and I did it quickly with the slash of my sword. He did not suffer."

I nodded and closed my eyes, letting his words soak in. A hollow, aching emptiness crept over me, replacing the anger that had burned within me little by little. I'd come to New Orleans for vengeance, but what I'd really needed were answers, and Belial had given those to me. Even if I didn't like them.

Belial's hand suddenly clasped mine, and my eyes snapped open. I took a shaky breath in, as I realized Belial wasn't the villain I'd painted him as. He'd made mistakes, just as my father had done, but he'd tried to make things right in the end...even if it had resulted in my father's death.

I wiped at my eyes as I asked, "But how did you become Death?"

He jerked his hand away from mine, his face going hard. "Once Fenrir was done, Death needed a new host, and we had no way to lock him up or send him to Void. He went after my sister, planning to possess her body, but she was just a baby." His voice shook a little, showing how much he cared for his sister. For *all* his family. "I told Death to take me instead, but after he possessed me, I was able to overcome the Elder God with the help of my family. I defeated him and became Death myself, instead of just a host body. And now I have to live with that for the rest of my life."

I sat on the bed, silent. My head was spinning with everything Belial had said. Grief settled over my shoulders like a shroud, but the burning need for vengeance was gone. My father had brought his death upon himself, and I had to accept that. I would always love him and miss him, but I could admit that he'd gone too far too.

"I didn't know," I said. "No one ever told me the whole story."

Belial stood up and crossed to the window, peering out at the darkening night sky. "It's not exactly a fun tale."

"No, but I should have known. He was my father and I loved him...but that doesn't mean he didn't make mistakes."

"We all did, and look where it got us." Belial turned back to me. "I never wanted to kill Fenrir, but I don't regret it either. I would do it again if I had to. Though we were once allies, we made our own choices and stood on opposite sides of the battle in the end." He moved to stand in front of me, towering over me with that strong, tall frame. "Now you must decide whether you want to stand against me too."

I stared up at him, my heart pounding wildly in my chest. A kaleidoscope of emotions flickered inside me, and I had no idea how to feel anymore. I'd once thought Belial was my enemy, but now he was my ally too. Would he become my enemy again when this was all over? And what about the overwhelming desire I felt for him whenever he was near?

But most of all, I worried that if I let go of the anger that consumed me, all that would be left was that aching emptiness—a loneliness and restlessness I had no way to fill.

"I haven't decided yet," I told Belial.

I stood and went to walk around Belial to grab my luggage, but he wrapped his hand around my upper arm to stop me. The point of contact flared icy-hot, and I stilled. When I tilted my head to look up at Belial, his lips were parted, as if on a word. That pull to lean in, to close the distance between us, struck me like a brick to the back of the skull. I swayed, and Belial's hand around my arm flexed and tightened minutely. It wasn't tight enough to hurt, and I could easily break out of it if I wanted, but I didn't want to.

"Eira," he whispered, and the sound of my name on his lips sent heat straight between my thighs. He said my name like it pained him, like he was desperate for something only I could help him with. "I don't want to be your enemy."

I didn't know how to answer that, especially when his other hand caressed my cheek, his thumb brushing against my lips, while he looked at me with so much need it actually burned. I was suddenly hyper-aware of the bed behind us, realizing Belial could easily throw me down on it. Did I want that? *Yes,* my mind whispered. *Take me. Take everything.*

I opened my mouth, not sure what exactly was going to come out of it, but before I could get a single word out, my phone chimed and the moment was broken. I shook myself free of Belial's hold, struggling to take a deep breath. *That was too close.*

I put some distance between us as I pulled my phone out of my pocket. A message had arrived from Loki. *I'm waiting at the bar for you.*

"Loki's downstairs waiting for me."

"That's convenient," Belial said, raising his eyebrows. "I didn't realize he was in town."

"Me either." I picked up my luggage, but Belial plucked it from my hands like it weighed nothing. If he was affected by what had just happened between us, I would never be able to tell. His face was completely impassive as he opened the door for me. Gone was the look of hunger in his eyes, and I found myself missing it.

I shook my head to clear it from those sorts of thoughts. I didn't have time to be thinking about Belial throwing me down on a bed and having his way with me, not when there were bigger problems to deal with, like stopping the Furies. It was time to focus on that, and I'd deal with the strange attraction between me and Belial later.

11

BELIAL

I grimaced as soon as I spotted Loki. It had been quite a few centuries since I'd seen him last, and even though his appearance had changed, he somehow hadn't changed at all. As an imp, he was a master of illusion and deception, and he was known as the world's greatest trickster for a reason. Somehow I doubted he'd become any more civilized since becoming an Archdemon either.

In his current form he had shiny black hair, perfect cheekbones, and a mischievous smile that never met his eyes. He lounged in a corner booth of the bar in an expensive suit, looking like he owned the place, but his eyes were watching everything, his clever brain always calculating.

Eira rushed toward Loki with an excited hop in her step, but I didn't bother hiding my dislike of the imp as we approached, letting the scowl show on my face.

In return, Loki looked at me like he'd come across a dead

fish in his house. "I'd say it's a pleasure," he said smoothly, "but I'd be lying."

"We both know that's what you're good at," I quipped back.

Loki's smile turned downright devious as we stared each other down. We had our reasons to hate each other. Back when I'd first tried to overthrow my father, Loki had been my friend and ally, and together we'd planned the coup against Lucifer. But right when I'd needed Loki the most, he'd betrayed me. At the very last minute he'd switched sides, warning Lucifer of the attack, including the team sneaking into the castle from the back. The team that had contained my first mate, Soria, who'd died that night before I could save her. All so Loki could save his own tail. Cowardly bastard.

But Loki had reason to hate me too. After all, I'd killed his son, Fenrir.

Eira stepped between us, breaking the rising tension before it could escalate into a fight, or something worse. "Thanks for meeting with us so quickly."

Loki's gaze snapped toward Eira and he rose to his feet to embrace her. "Eira, darling. Always lovely to see you."

For a split second, I watched his face soften. Even if he didn't like me, hopefully his love for Eira would be enough to compensate. From that look alone, I knew that it wasn't likely that he would trick his own granddaughter.

"Sit and have a drink with me," Loki said, gesturing at

the table. Eira slid into the booth across from him, and I grudgingly scooted in beside her.

"What are you doing here?" I asked, trying to keep the hostility out of my voice. I'd expected that he'd call her, not show up out of the blue at my father's hotel.

"When I didn't hear from Eira after I sent her on this mission, I came to New Orleans to make sure she was okay," he said, tilting his chin up at me like he was daring me to question it.

"Is that right?" I asked, meeting his gaze head on. I didn't believe him for a second. If he was in the city, why hadn't he contacted her sooner, or reached out first? If there was one thing Loki was good at it was lying, and he would do it more often than telling the truth.

But Eira didn't seem bothered by his answer and shot me an exasperated look. "Be nice," she muttered.

"Let me get you some drinks," Loki said, breaking my stare first. It didn't feel like a win. "You both look like you need some."

"Good idea," Eira said.

Loki flagged down the server and we ordered our drinks, before he spoke again. "What have you found out so far?"

"I found my brothers. They're alive, along with the other shifters and imps that went missing, but they're not exactly safe." She bit her lip and glanced at me, like she wasn't sure if she should keep going.

"What do you mean?" Loki asked.

"Two of the Furies are here," I said. "Alecto and

Megaera. They're trying to bring Tisiphone over from Void next."

Loki's eyes widened slightly. "The Furies? That's...unexpected."

"They're gathering together shifters and imps like cultists, putting them under some sort of spell, using anger and envy to control them," Eira said, rubbing her hands over her arms as if she was cold. I had the sudden urge to wrap my arms around her, to protect her from whatever was bothering her, whether it was a chill in the bar or the memories in her head.

"I see," Loki said, frowning as he tapped his fingers slowly on the side of his drink. "Anger and envy. Yes, of course."

"They need to be stopped," I said. "You know what kind of damage they can cause."

"Yes, I remember," Loki said, giving me a hard look.

"We need to send the Furies back to Void, but we don't have a key," Eira said. "That's why I contacted you."

"Of course," Loki said, leaning back with an amused grin. "And lucky you did, because I doubt anyone else could help you with this problem."

"Do you have one?" Eira asked, sitting up straighter.

"No, but I did once. I hid it in Faerie to keep it safe." He tilted his head. "I can't get to it, but perhaps you can."

"How?" I asked.

Loki shot me another amused glance. "Eira has a key to Faerie. Didn't you know?"

I gritted my teeth. It took pretty much all of my

willpower to not punch that smug look off of his thin, foxy face. "No, she failed to mention it."

Eira shrugged. "I used to be a messenger between Earth and Faerie, and I still have a key. There was no reason to mention it before since it was here at the hotel."

"But surely an Archdemon such as yourself can get to Faerie too," I said, giving Loki a pointed look. "There must be another reason you need us to get the key."

"Well, there is one tiny little complication," he admitted.

"Here we go," I muttered.

Loki ignored my comment as he continued. "I left it in a cave with a basilisk for safekeeping. The beast can see through illusion magic, which is why I can't get it myself. Of course that also means that no fae can get to it either, especially since it can kill with a single glance. A perfect hiding spot, don't you think?"

I narrowed my eyes at him. "If it can see through your illusion magic, how did you get it there in the first place?"

"I had help." Loki smiled mysteriously at me. I expected him to elaborate, but in his typical, slippery manner, he didn't say more.

Eira cleared her throat. "Okay, so it's in a cave with a basilisk that you can't get past because it sees through your illusion magic and can kill with a look. What makes you think we can get past it?"

"Because you have the God of Death sitting here with you. It shouldn't be an issue for him."

"And what do you want in return?" I asked, because

obviously Loki wanted something. He wouldn't help us unless it benefited him in some way.

His smile turned predatory. "I'll tell you where the cave is, as long as you give me the key once you're done with it."

Eira opened her mouth, but I put a hand on her arm to stop her. There was no way I was getting Loki a key to Void. I said one simple word: "No."

"It's mine anyway," Loki said, waving his hand idly. "I'm simply letting you borrow it for a while."

"Yeah, after we go on a deadly mission to retrieve it for you." I snorted. "How do I know you won't turn around and use it on me the moment we hand it over?"

"Are you worried I'll send you to Void for killing my son?" Loki asked, voice carefully neutral.

Eira looked between us, her jaw clenched. She still didn't know how to feel about me, even after learning the whole story, and I wasn't sure she'd defend me from Loki if he tried.

"It wasn't personal," I gritted out.

"You of all people should know that death is always personal," Loki said, and his voice took on a sharper tone.

Touché, I thought. I met his gaze and stared him down again. This time the tension rose even higher, crackling through the air like lightning, and Eira's presence beside us wasn't enough to stop it.

She blew out a breath. "If you two are done having a dick measuring contest, we still have things to resolve."

Loki sat back, folding his hands on the table. "I give my word not to use the Void key against you if you give it to me.

But I can't speak for Eira, of course. If she wants to use it, I won't stop her." He seemed wickedly delighted by the idea of Eira using the key against me.

"Fine," I ground out. "I agree to give you the key once we're done with it. If it survives the encounter, of course."

Loki frowned, as if he hadn't expected that, and his eye twitched. But I'd learned long ago it was always wise to go above and beyond when bargaining with the trickster.

"Very well," Loki said. "I give you my word."

"Your word's not good enough," I growled. "We tried that once, or don't you remember? I want blood."

Loki rolled his eyes. "You're always so dramatic."

He pulled out a small knife from his suit and cut his hand, before he passed it to me. I slashed my skin in the same spot, and we clasped hands and met eyes.

"I swear on my blood," I said, and Loki repeated the words. Power surged between us as we nodded, our bargain struck.

"Excellent," Loki said, as he released my hand and used a napkin to wipe the blood off himself.

"Where exactly do we go in Faerie?" Eira asked.

"I'll draw you a map."

"Good," I said. "Then Eira can open up the portal, and I'll go through alone and get the key."

Eira's gaze snapped to me. "No fucking way. I'm going too."

"It's not safe for you." My chest tightened at the thought of Eira facing down a basilisk. Unlike me, she wouldn't be immune to its killing gaze, and I was worried about her going up against it. I hated the idea of her being in danger. Why was I so worried about her? Wasn't she about two decisions away from stabbing me in the back? But there was something that connected us. *Are you my mate?*

Eira snorted. "When was the last time you were in Faerie? You need me to navigate the place. You'll never get to this cave without me."

"She has a point," Loki said.

I shot him a glare, and then downed my forgotten drink. Faerie was notoriously difficult to navigate, and I'd never been a fan of the place. Plus, other than that brief trip with my mother to free Famine, I hadn't been there in years. "Fine. But you'll do what I say when we fight the basilisk."

"Deal. *If* you take these damn cuffs off of me first." She shook her wrist in front of me, the silver of the cuffs catching the light.

Oh right, the cuffs. There was a good chance that the moment I took them off she'd be right back to flinging ice spears into my back again, but we needed her magic in Faerie. Could I trust her? I wasn't sure, even though something in my gut told me to give her a chance.

"Fine," I snapped. "But as part of that deal, you agree to stop trying to kill me."

"Oh, please do keep trying to kill him," Loki said, his eyes sparkling with mirth.

"I haven't tried to kill you since that first time," Eira said, raising her eyes to the ceiling in exasperation.

"Only because you haven't had the chance to try again," I said.

"I agree to stop trying to kill you. Happy? Or do we need to seal our deal in blood too?"

"I don't think that's necessary."

Loki chuckled as he watched the two of us argue. "If that's settled, I'll make you a map."

He grabbed a napkin and unfolded it, then waved his hand over it. The napkin turned to an elaborately drawn paper map that looked like it was a few hundred years old, featuring a big red X over a cave. I looked it over, but had no idea what most of the landmarks were, or where to even begin. Eira, on the other hand, gave it a quick glance and nodded, proving that I did need her after all.

"We'll let you know when we're done with the key," I told Loki, as I slid out of the booth, eager to be done with this meeting. "If we survive."

Loki stood too and his green eyes glowed slightly. "You'd better be sure Eira does, or I *will* destroy you," he said in a low, dangerous voice. "I don't care if you're an Elder God. I'll find a way."

Interesting. It seemed the self-serving imp actually cared for his granddaughter. Not enough to come with us, of course, but enough to throw idle threats my way.

Eira rose to her feet and tucked the map into her luggage. "I'll be fine. I can take care of myself, you know."

"I know you can, darling." Loki gave her a warm smile. "After all, you were trained by the best. Me."

I rolled my eyes so hard it almost hurt, then grabbed Eira's arm and practically dragged her out of there. She called out a 'thanks' to Loki as we headed outside, and then she glared at me, no doubt annoyed by my rudeness. Like I gave a fuck. I wasn't spending one more second in that trickster's presence if I could help it.

"See, I told you he wasn't so bad," Eira said, while I flagged down the valet.

"You call that 'not bad?'" I asked with a snort.

"For Loki, yeah. Trust me, he can be so much worse."

"I'm familiar," I said dryly. "We go way back."

"Right. I forget you're an old man sometimes. Must be the tattoos."

The valet brought my car around in record time, making me wonder if he knew who I was. Probably. Many people said I looked like a rougher, more muscular version of my father. I didn't see it though. I preferred to think I took after Eve in most ways. Except for my pride—that was all Lucifer.

I put Eira's luggage in the trunk and opened the door for her, before getting in myself. Night had fallen across the city, and this would normally be when my intense hunger to steal souls from the living rose up and became unbearable. Yet ever since meeting Eira it had lain dormant, or been replaced by hunger for her. The relief was palpable, but I wondered how long it would last.

"We should wait until the morning to go to Faerie," Eira said, while I drove. "It'll be a bit of a journey through Faerie to get to the cave."

I nodded. "You'll stay at the bar or my apartment tonight. I have some things to do."

"Like roaming the streets as a vigilante?"

"Maybe." That shifter from last night was still out there,

though I was less excited about killing him now that I knew he was being controlled by the Furies. That had to be why more and more people were being attacked throughout the city—the Furies were inciting anger and jealousy, first in shifters and imps, and then in other people too. Stopping them would end a lot of the violence in New Orleans.

"I'm coming with you," she said.

"No." I wanted to test what happened if I put some distance between us. Would my hunger for death return? "I need to be alone tonight. And I think you do too. You learned a lot today about your father and you need time to process it all." I looked over at her, but she was staring out the window, her pretty little chin jutted forward stubbornly. "Grieve tonight, fight tomorrow."

She drew in a long breath and met my eyes, then nodded. "Grieve tonight. Fight tomorrow."

12

EIRA

Belial abandoned me in his bar, and though I was tempted to go after him, his words about needing to be alone had struck a chord in me. I decided to give him some space, partly because I needed it too. When I was around him my emotions were too raw and my head spun with conflicting thoughts. He'd killed my father—he'd admitted as much, and even said he'd had no regrets about it. I tried to be mad about that, to hold onto the simmering anger inside me, but it sounded like my father had lost himself to Death by that point. By defeating him, Belial had helped stop the fourth Horseman from going all apocalyptic on the world. I would always miss my father and wish he were still alive now, but I also had to accept that he had gone too far and needed to be stopped. I only wished my brothers had been more honest about what had happened.

Of course, Belial could be lying, but somehow I knew in my gut he wasn't. His story matched up with bits and pieces

I'd seen and heard myself, and had filled in a lot of holes in my knowledge about what had happened. As much as I hated trusting him, something inside me told me he was telling the truth.

But where did we go from here?

"What'll it be?" Yumi asked, bringing me out of my thoughts.

When Belial had left me in the bar, he'd told Yumi I could order any food and drinks on the house. Then he'd warned me not to leave the building, if I wanted to get my cuffs off. Proving he was still an asshole.

"Rum and coke, please." I stared down at the menu in front of me. "And the Cajun pizza."

"Good choice," Yumi said.

She put in my order and then went to make my drink, while I watched her. She moved with the grace of a supernatural, and I wondered what exactly she was and how she'd come to work here for Belial.

"Do you have any idea where Belial went?" I asked, as she slid the drink toward me.

"It's better not to ask," Yumi said with a wry grin.

"Does he do this a lot?"

She nodded as she ran a cloth over the bar. "He slips out every night, usually between serving up drinks at the bar. He's gone about an hour or two, and when he comes back he usually looks...different."

I leaned forward. "Different how?"

She cocked her head as she considered. "I don't know.

Better. More refreshed. Like he's just woken from a really good nap.

"Somehow I doubt that's what he's doing," I muttered. "Does he ever come back injured or anything?"

Her eyes narrowed. "Trying to find a weakness? Trust me, he doesn't have one."

"No, just curious." I took a long sip of my drink as I eyed her up. "Are the two of you an item or something?"

She let out a sharp laugh. "Me and Belial? No way. For one thing, he's my boss." Her eyes flashed with amusement. "For another thing, you're more my type than he is."

I couldn't help but feel a wave of relief. "Sorry. You just seem really protective of him."

She lifted one shoulder in a casual shrug. "I guess because he's protective of me too. He's like a big brother. Not just to me, but to all Nephilim."

Nephilim was the term used for anyone who was half human, and half angel or Fallen. Like Belial had been, before he'd become Death. "How so?"

Yumi leaned on the counter. "Many years ago, when Heaven and Hell were still at war, Belial set up a network here on Earth to help and support the Nephilim. Back then, our kind were all outcasts thanks to our half-human blood, but there were more and more being born every year. Belial took in everyone, whether they were part angel or Fallen, saying that Nephilim were neutral and not on either side of that pointless war. He gave them food, clothes, shelter, jobs, and whatever else he could." She refilled my drink, which I hadn't realized had gone empty. "Nowadays things have changed, of course. Angels and demons have called a truce, and over the last few years they've started to become more accepting of Nephilim. But Belial still runs the network and makes sure anyone in need gets help. He just does a lot of it on the internet now. We have a Facebook group and everything."

"I had no idea," I said, staring into my drink. Every single thing I learned about Belial changed my perception of him a little bit, making me doubt that he truly was the villain of my story.

Yumi disappeared into the back room, and then returned with my Cajun pizza, which smelled divine. The bar was starting to pick up as it grew later, and she wandered off to take some more orders while I ate, but then she returned, like she wanted to talk to me some more. At least she wasn't openly hostile anymore.

"How did you meet Belial?" I asked, before devouring another slice of pizza.

"For most of my life, I thought I was human and had no idea the supernatural world existed. When my wings sprouted, I panicked. My parents did too." She picked up a peanut from a little jar and popped it in her mouth. "Turns out my mom had a one night stand with a Fallen angel back in the day, and I was a result of that. It tore my family apart and I ran away, feeling like I was losing my mind and terrified of the changes happening in my body. Belial heard about me somehow and tracked me down in Oklahoma. He took me in, explained the entire supernatural world to me, and helped me learn to control my powers. He even got me enrolled in Hellspawn Academy and found my biological dad, who had no idea I even existed." Her eyes took on a faraway look as she tossed a few more peanuts in her mouth. "But I never really fit in at Hellspawn Academy, being a half-blood and all. So when I graduated, I came back to New Orleans and asked Belial for a job. Now this is my home."

"I'm sorry you went through all that," I said. "I know what it's like not to fit in anywhere either. I'm half fae and half demon."

She nodded. "It's hard, isn't it? Always straddling the line between two worlds, and never fully belonging in either. But I found my place here, and with the other Nephilim I have a new family." She gave me another wry grin. "Maybe Belial will help you find your place too."

"If he ever comes back," I muttered, which got an amused chuckle out of her.

"Oh, he will. I have a feeling he won't want you out of sight for long."

She moved away to help other customers, and I finished off my pizza while the bar grew more and more crowded. When I was finished I gave a little wave to Yumi, and then headed up the stairs to Belial's apartment. He'd given me my own access code and I punched it in now, then slipped inside and flipped on the lights. For a few seconds I simply stared at the space, taking it all in without his distracting presence at my side. Without Belial's energy dominating the room, it seemed a lot less imposing.

I decided to do a little snooping, telling myself he must

have known I would do it. Who wouldn't? I checked out every single room, hoping to find some dirty secrets tucked away somewhere, but his place was surprisingly well organized, with very little clutter. I'd met immortals before who had a whole collection of stuff stored away in rooms and warehouses. People who liked stuff and were able to keep it forever? They took hoarding to a new level. But not Belial.

Belial still had a few interesting artifacts, but to my surprise, they were kept to the minimum—a few pieces of ancient Greek pottery, a small box of old jewelry from different eras, an old voodoo doll in the corner of his office, and a few other small things here and there. I wondered what the stories behind each of them were, but didn't find anything too shocking. He also had a vast array of first edition books from all sorts of important people. I flipped through a few, but mostly kept my hands off them, just in case they crumbled apart in my fingers. He had kept most of them in excellent condition, but there was only so much a book could take after existing for hundreds of years. I'd heard that Lucifer had one of the most impressive libraries in the world, and Belial seemed to have a miniature version here. It made me think he was more like his father than he cared to admit.

The most disturbing thing about the apartment was how little food there was in the kitchen. The man really didn't need to eat. Although I did find a bag of fancy chocolates, which I plucked from the shelf and ate as I wandered around the apartment some more. He'd told me to eat whatever I wanted, after all.

When I was done with my search I got ready for bed, grateful to have my own clothes and all my toiletries again. Then I found myself staring down at Belial's bed, at the dark gray sheets where he'd been sleeping naked last night. No, not sleeping. He didn't need to sleep either. So why should he get the bed while I was forced to sleep on his uncomfortable couch? Would he even be back tonight? I had no idea. It seemed a damn shame to let the bed go to waste, especially when it looked so comfortable. I'd doze off a little, and then move back to the couch before he got home.

The sheets caressed my skin like silk, and the pillow was the perfect blend of hard and soft. Plus it all smelled like Belial, even without my wolf senses (damn these cuffs), which made me only sink into the bed even more. No one would know, I told myself, as I drifted off to sleep.

I woke to the sound of Belial's deep voice. "What are you doing in my bed?"

Damn. Busted.

In that moment I had a choice—scrabble up and act embarrassed, or just fucking own it. So I did the latter. "It's more comfortable than the couch," I said with a yawn and a shrug. "No one else was using it."

Belial's eyes tracked my every movement with obvious hunger. "If you want in my bed so badly, I'd be happy to invite you."

The sultry tone of his voice left nothing to the imagination, and heat flooded me at the naughty images it conjured. I found my eyes wandering over him too. He wasn't wearing his hooded cloak, and the black t-shirt showed off all his muscles and tattoos. I'd already had a glimpse of what was underneath those clothes too and my mouth watered at the thought of another peek.

I dragged my eyes away. "Not if you're in it with me."

He took a step forward. "We both know that's not true."

Before he climbed in with me, I hopped out of his of bed. I wore only a little silk nightgown that left little to the imagination, and I put some distance between us quickly before we both got any ideas in our heads. Maybe a change of subject would help. "Where have you been?"

"I went hunting, but couldn't find that shifter from last night. It's possible the Furies are having them be more cautious or staying out of the city now that they know we're on to them."

"So no killing spree last night for the Grim Reaper of New Orleans? You must be disappointed."

He gave me a villainous smile. "No, the Grim Reaper was alive and well last night, protecting the city as best he could."

"Did you kill anyone?" I asked, a shiver running down my spine.

His eyes darkened and his voice turned hard. "I found a woman stabbed nearly to death, and a man about to rape her. I quickly dealt with him and then flew her to the hospital. I believe she made it. He did not. I feel no guilt about that."

I bit my lip and looked away, unable to chastise him for what he'd done. I'd have done the same thing if I'd been there.

"That took all night?" The words slipped out, and I wondered if I was starting to lose my mind. When had I turned into his nagging woman? And why did I care what he did with his time?

"I had to...test a theory." His eyes swept over me again with a frown. "I also went grocery shopping."

"Oh yeah, I noticed your kitchen was totally empty."

His lips turned up in amusement. "I don't need much, but you do. But I wasn't sure what you liked, so I got all sorts of things. Next time you can make me a list."

A pang hit my chest. "You did that for me?"

He shrugged. "You need to eat. And starting today you're no longer my prisoner, but my guest."

Excitement hummed through me at his words, and I gazed down at my silver cuffs. I couldn't wait to get them off, or to go back to Faerie, which I hadn't visited in over a year.

"Come on. I'll make you something to eat." He turned and walked out of the bedroom, and I watched his fine ass as he went.

I couldn't help myself.

13

EIRA

I quickly took a shower and got dressed, donning my combat leathers because you could never be too careful in Faerie. Besides, most of my other clothes would stick out there. The fae were definitely not jeans and t-shirts kind of people.

I was drawn back to the kitchen by the smell of food cooking. Belial was making a feast of eggs, bacon, and pancakes, and it was all for me. Unbelievable. Why couldn't he just let me keep hating him? No, he had to go and be nice to me, all while being so freaking hot it was hard to take my eyes off him. Asshole.

"Breakfast will be ready in a few minutes," he said.

I nodded and glanced at the map sitting on the bar counter. Loki had made it yesterday with his illusion magic, and I wondered how long it would hold. You'd never know by looking at it that it had once been a simple bar napkin. It even felt like old parchment paper when I picked it up to examine it again. The basilisk cave was located in Summer Court territory, which I wasn't thrilled about, but if we were lucky I could get us there without encountering many fae. As a messenger, I'd been all over the place in Faerie, and I knew all the landmarks Loki had mapped out for me. It should be pretty easy to get to, or so I hoped.

Belial served me up a plate of food, and I had to admit he was a good cook. He saved only a single piece of bacon for himself, explaining that it was one of the few things he missed the taste of. I couldn't blame him. I devoured my food quickly, eager to get moving, while he took a fast shower and got dressed.

When he returned, he held a small silver wand in his hand. "Let's get this over with."

He made a motion for me to give him my hands, and when he touched the little wand to my silver cuffs, they snapped open immediately. My power rushed back in, and it was almost overwhelming as it poured back into me all at once. I breathed in deep and let it settle until I felt complete again, and fully *me* once more. But just to be sure, I formed a ball of ice in one hand and turned my fingers to claws on the other. I was *back*.

I looked up at Belial with a smile on my lips, but he was watching me closely with narrowed eyes, like he expected me to whip out another ice sword and stab him. I didn't, of course. No, if I was going to try that again, I'd wait until he was caught off guard. But I was starting to doubt my plan to kill him a little more every day.

"Much better," I said, as I banished my claws and ice,

then rubbed my wrists where the cuffs had been. My body instantly healed any bruising or soreness there, now that my magic was back, but I still let out a soft sigh, so relieved to have them gone.

"Ready to go?" Belial asked, and I nodded.

Together we threw some food, water, extra clothes, and some other necessities into a heavy outdoor backpack, which Belial strapped to his back. Then I dug around in a secret compartment of my luggage and removed a necklace there, with a round polished gemstone with a rainbow of colors moving inside of it. The key to Faerie. Even though I hadn't used it in over a year, I always kept it close to me. It was one of the few things I had left from my mother.

"Stand back," I said, as I clutched the gem and called upon my fae power to open the portal, picturing the location in my mind of where I wanted to go. A beam of colorful light burst out of the stone and expanded into a glowing, swirling portal, just large enough for us to pass through one at a time. I stared at the myriad of colors swirling in front of me, before turning to Belial. "Let's go."

"Ladies first."

"Don't worry, I didn't open the portal into a death trap," I muttered. But just so he knew it was safe, I stepped through first.

Belial's living room faded away as soon as I got to the other side of the portal, which took me to the edge of the Summer Court territory, to a forest I knew would be safe to enter without being noticed. I inhaled the sharp scent of the trees here, which were bursting with purple flowers that gave off a vibrant fragrance. All the colors seemed brighter here too, from the grass at our feet to the bright blue sky above us. It was a cool morning with a hint of chill in the air with the promise of a warmer afternoon. Of course, the seasons were different here in Faerie—all four of them played out across the space of a single day. Judging by the current temperature, I guessed we had arrived at the early spring portion of the day, with summer a few hours ahead of us, when it would get much hotter before settling into autumn before returning to winter in the evening.

It's been too long, I thought, as I looked around while Belial stepped through the portal. I was excited to be back in Faerie, even if it wasn't the Winter Court where I came from. I'd been to the Summer Court plenty of times while playing messenger, but I longed for the snowy, frost-ridden lands that held the key to my powers. Plus I had my own reasons for avoiding the Summer Court as much as possible.

Meanwhile, Belial squinted in the bright light as if it was hurting his eyes. I grinned at how out of place he looked here, even though I was sure he must have been to Faerie many times before during his long life.

I glanced down at Loki's map to check my bearings. "We're going to try to avoid encountering any fae," I said, before setting off through the trees.

"Works for me," Belial said, as he kept pace with me. "How long has it been since you were last here?"

"A little over a year."

"Do you miss it?"

"Sometimes. Being a messenger to Faerie gave me a

purpose, at least. A chance to prove my mixed heritage was useful in some way."

"Did you grow up here?" he asked.

I was surprised by all his questions. Was he really interested in hearing all this? "No, my mother was killed by a rival in the Summer Court when I was a baby, and I don't remember her at all. I grew up mostly with Fenrir and my brothers on Earth, but I visited my Winter Court family members a lot as a child. But I've never really been accepted as either a shifter or a fae, but always as something in between."

"I get that," Belial said. "I was the first Nephilim, the product of Lucifer falling for the human woman Eve. It was quite scandalous at the time."

"I bet. Half-breeds are still not totally accepted among any supernaturals, but it made me a good messenger between the fae and demons. Well, at least until my father decided to go and start a civil war among the demons to try and overthrow Lucifer. That ended my messenger days."

"Would you ever go back to being a messenger?"

"I don't know," I said honestly. "It's what I'm good at and it's probably the best job for me, since I don't really fit in with either world."

"I understand where you're coming from," Belial said. "I was cast out from Hell a long time ago and sent to live on Earth long before most other angels or demons came here. I've done my best to make it my home though, and to help others like me."

I slanted a glance at him. "Yes, Yumi told me about your

network of Nephilim, and about how you helped her out. And helped many others, it sounds like."

"I do what I can," Belial said with a shrug. "I know how hard it is to be alone and confused and unsure where your place is in the world, so I created a network for people like me, who can help each other out so none of us is every truly alone."

"Very noble," I said, almost grudgingly. "Yumi speaks very highly of you."

"She had a difficult time, but I tried to help her out as best I could. She's one of the younger Nephilim around. Now that angels and demons live on Earth, there are more half-humans than ever, and I want them all to not have to struggle like I did."

Something warm erupted in my chest as he spoke about Yumi and the others like a proud papa. He really did understand what it was like being an outcast, and I had the sudden feeling that we understood each other more than we originally thought.

Then it hit me—I *liked* him. Not because of his deadly good looks, or because of whatever desire tied us together. We had more in common than I wanted to admit, and I'd discovered he wasn't a total villain, but someone trying to make the world a better place however he could. Plus he kept trying to help me out too, even though I'd tried to kill him. Shit. Was I developing *feelings* for him? This wasn't supposed to happen at all. We were enemies, and I'd come to New Orleans to kill him. I'd only agreed to team up with him temporarily to find the missing shifters while also looking for a weakness in him. But it wasn't as simple as that anymore.

We lapsed into a comfortable silence for a while, simply walking through the forest, and Belial's shadows concealed us anytime we got too close to other fae. I checked the map frequently to make sure we were on course, and made slight alterations to make sure that we'd be staying out of the way of any large towns. As we traveled, the weather warmed up very quickly, and it was brutally hot by midday.

I'd nearly forgotten how intense the Summer Court's day could be. It would start cooling off soon though as it switched to fall and then winter, although it would stay warm enough for us to sleep outside at least. That was one good thing the Summer Court had going for it. The only thing, I thought darkly as I wiped my brow against the seemingly endless streams of sweat dripping down my forehead. Demons were not meant for the heat, and neither were Winter Court fae, which meant I suffered doubly for it. For some time I shifted into wolf form and ran while Belial flew overhead, which helped for a while, but we had to be careful that no one saw us like that. That was the same reason we didn't ride Ghost, even though it would have been faster and easier—the fae might have been able to sense his otherworldly presence in this realm. There would be too many questions if we were caught by the fae here, and we didn't have time for that.

It turned cooler as the sun set and the winter night set in. Eventually Belial and I stopped to camp for the night in a clearing that looked like it had been used by other travelers, judging by the remains of a campfire. Luckily Belial and I wouldn't need one of those tonight, as neither of us was bothered by the cold.

I gratefully sat down on a fallen log once we were settled and stretched my aching legs. It had been quite some time since I'd covered so much ground in one day and I was unused to it. I was looking forward to getting some sleep, although we'd have to take turns keeping watch to make sure no one came upon us while we were asleep.

Belial rummaged around in his backpack and then passed me a little brown bag. "Here. You need to eat something."

I raised my eyebrows as I caught it and checked inside, finding a sandwich and a bag of chips that he must have packed for me. Fuck, why was he so nice to me? I wished he would stop. Okay, not really, because I was pretty hungry, and I appreciated him thinking of me, but he really was making it hard to dislike him. "Thank you. Are you going to eat anything?"

"No, I'll be fine. I also don't need sleep, so you can rest as much as you want. I'll keep watch the whole night."

"Must be nice," I said. "What's it like being an Elder God?"

Belial watched me for a few moments, his eyes inscrutable in the low light. "I wouldn't wish it on anyone," he finally said, in a brutally honest tone.

I hadn't expected an answer like that from him, especially since he'd flaunted to me so many times that he couldn't be killed. "Why not? You're so powerful. Like seriously overpowered. You've said it so many times, that you're unkillable. Isn't that the best thing?"

"I suppose."

"I'm sensing a 'but.'"

"But the cost of such power..." he trailed off and shook his head.

"What cost?" I asked, holding my breath.

"It doesn't matter." He looked down at his hands, his voice hollow and his face stark. "Try to get some sleep."

I huffed at his dismissal. Why had he piqued my interest like that just to back down at the last second? He was being worse than Loki, but I had the feeling that he wouldn't take kindly to that comparison. "You can tell me, you know."

"Maybe another time."

"Stubborn ass," I muttered.

Belial just chuckled softly as I shifted into wolf form and settled on the ground in a softer patch of dirt. It was easier to sleep outside as a wolf, although I still moved around uncomfortably for a bit. It had been a while since I'd slept out under the stars like this.

I closed my eyes, but cracked them back open when Belial scuffed the ground standing up. He looked down at me with dark eyes as he draped his cloak over the ground and patted for me to lie on it. I hesitated only a second, before scooting over onto the thick fabric, but turned around so he couldn't see my face as the confusion inside me surged. The cloak smelled like him, and it was especially strong with my wolf nose. I tried to resist the urge to inhale for several moments, but then I gave up and breathed it in. I smelled traces of alcohol, leather, blood, and metal, but mostly the unmistakable scent of *him*. Something I knew I'd always be able to find now, and would never forget. I wanted to push the cloak away from me, to remind him that we were enemies and he had no business offering up his clothes like we were friends...or more. But I couldn't do it. Instead I just snuggled a bit closer, finally growing comfortable, while hating that I liked this so much, even as I fell asleep with his smell in my head.

14

BELIAL

We got to the cave the next morning and hid in some bushes while we scoped out the situation. The cave appeared to be larger than I expected, and I got the feeling it extended far into the mountain behind it. Beside me, Eira stared intently at the entrance, eyes narrowed as if she was listening very hard for something. With her shifter senses, she could probably hear things I couldn't.

She glanced over at me. "I don't hear much. It might be asleep."

"I don't think that matters," I said. "It will probably wake up."

"I know that," Eira snapped. She seemed very irritated this morning, but I couldn't figure out why. When she'd woken up, she'd been in a bad mood, and I wished she would just tell me why instead of giving me the silent treatment.

We hadn't talked on the rest of the journey to the cave, except to discuss the plan. I would distract the basilisk since I was more likely to survive going toe to toe with it than Eira. Meanwhile, Eira would sneak into the cave and get the key. Then we'd get the fuck out of there as fast as we could, because basilisks were damn near impossible to kill, and I wasn't looking to try today.

I held out the scrap of cloth I'd crafted into a makeshift blindfold. Eira eyed it, curling her lips. "Are you sure I have to wear that?" she asked. "This would be a lot easier if I could see."

"You don't need to see. You can use your other senses to navigate the cave, and this is the best way to avoid accidentally looking at the basilisk on the way."

We'd already agreed on this plan, so she was stalling putting it on. I knew how much she hated the idea, but it was the only way I was letting her participate. I didn't care what she said—if she met the basilisk's eyes, even accidentally, she'd be dead. No fucking way was I letting that happen. For some reason I couldn't explain, her safety suddenly mattered more to me than anything else.

"Fine," Eira said with a heavy sigh. She shifted into her wolf form, and I crouched down. Her white shoulders tensed as I slipped the fabric over her eyes and tied it as tightly as I could without hurting her. My fingers brushed the thick fur at the nape of her neck, and I had to physically resist the urge to dig my fingers in and pet her. The strong, inexplicable pull dragged me toward her once again, and the never-ending hunger for death was sated whenever she was around, fading into nothing. It was only temporary though, as I'd discovered the other night when I'd gone out in the city on my own and put some distance between us. Still, she was the only thing I had found that could take it away. I closed my eyes and basked in the feeling for just a moment before I forced myself to pull away.

"Can you see?" I asked.

She moved her white head around, ears twitching forward to track my voice. She shook her head in a very humanoid movement. I watched her test her paws, stepping around a bush and then circling back around to face me dead center, while a pit formed in my stomach. Worry. Something I hadn't felt in such a long time. I wanted to protect her from everything, but she had insisted that she be part of it. I understood why—she didn't trust me at all. In her mind, if I went in the cave, there was a good chance that I wouldn't be coming back out to help her. I wasn't sure how to convince her otherwise.

She started to turn toward the cave, but I called after her. "Eira, wait."

She stopped dead in her tracks, her ears perking up. I reached forward, and she flinched slightly as I threaded my hand in the fur on top of her head and rubbed her lightly. Eira bared her teeth at me and let a low growl, but she didn't move away. Instead, she lightly pushed her head against my hand, as if she couldn't help herself. She'd never admit it to me, but I could tell she liked my touch.

After a moment, she snapped at my fingers with her teeth and yanked herself away. She disappeared into the plants we were currently hiding behind. I looked on with a heavy heart as I watched her fluffy white tail disappear into the distance.

Now it was time to work my magic. I couldn't focus for too long on Eira because I had to make sure I could lure out the basilisk so she could sneak in and get the key. I closed my eyes and cracked my knuckles. I sent feelers out, not surprised to find lots and lots of death in the area. To my deathly senses, it was like a beacon around the cave, lighting it up like the Vegas Strip at night.

I raised my hands and let the power of Death run through me. Most of the time I tried to keep this part of me locked away, sealed up to protect the living around me, and to keep the hunger contained as long as I could. Now I let it rush through me, such unfathomable power that it made me tremble, and I knew my eyes would be glowing purple, as they did when I tapped into the power of Death. I was an Elder God, one of the fundamental elements of the universe, unkillable and all-powerful, and for a moment I reveled in it. This much power was incredible, though it definitely didn't make up for the overwhelming hunger for stealing life I felt all the time. Until Eira, anyway.

The dead reacted to me like I'd rung a dinner bell, and started waking up slowly. It was sluggish for some of them, the ones who had been here for a long time, but many of the bodies were more recent. I was fairly sure they'd all tried to enter the cave before meeting their fate. Whether they knew what was inside or not, none of them had made it very far.

The newer bodies dragged themselves out of the ground, their movements jerky and unnatural. The older ones had been ground to pieces by time and dirt, but they reformed from the dust as skeletons, their bones creaking as they moved. Soon my army of the dead stood before me, with over two dozen of them. I nodded once, pleased with my handiwork. It should be enough to draw the attention of the basilisk.

"Go make some noise," I ordered.

The dead fae soldiers turned as one, walking over to the mouth of the cave. They rattled and chattered like a storm of the damned, and I focused on commanding them to be as loud as possible. For a few minutes, they raged on with no sign of anything from the cave. Then there was a loud roar, and a dark shape filled the entrance.

The basilisk was one of the more terrifying creatures I'd encountered before, and that was saying something. The back end of it was a giant serpent, the tail twisting far into the cave, but in front it looked like a rooster, with a giant pointy beak and sharp talons on its two feet, along with some feathered wings that didn't look big enough to actually lift the creature. I suspected it wasn't very good at actually flying, but that didn't matter when it had ten other ways to kill you.

The basilisk knocked the undead soldiers aside like they were nothing more than toys. They fell back to dust and the basilisk let out a huge roar, swiveling its huge head around to look for the source of the magic. I tossed a ball of blue hell-fire in its direction, and just like that, I had the complete attention of one of the most deadly creatures on the planet solely on me. It's eyes locked on me, but nothing happened. At least Loki had been right about the death gaze not affecting me.

I volleyed a few more hellfire balls at the basilisk, which only seemed to piss it off. It crept out after me as I drew back from the cave, yelling and waving my arms above my head, trying to keep its attention solely on me as I used shadow magic and hellfire against it. It didn't seem phased by either, and started acting like it was going to head back into the cave.

Damn, what did it take to injure this thing? I'd have to step up my game if I wanted to get it out of the cave so Eira could sneak inside. I needed to make myself such a delectable target that it wouldn't be able to resist. It was just parrying my blows, looking generally annoyed, but not threatened enough to leave it's home to come after me.

I unfurled my wings and took flight to swoop above the basilisk, hitting it with hellfire from a new angle. It watched me, interest piqued as I flew above, and then it blew a long, hot blast of fire. I gritted my teeth and dodged, swooping off to the side so the fire shot straight into the sky.

Well, fuck. There could be dozens of nearby fae who had seen that fire, and I was betting they'd be here soon to try and figure out what was going on at the cave with the basilisk. We needed to get in, get the key, and get out as quickly as possible, so no one would learn why we were here.

I grimaced and dove down again, swooping in a bit closer, narrowly dodging a claw that went after me before trying again. It was dangerous to do this when the thing could move so fast. If I wasn't careful, it could swipe me out of the air, or grab me and swallow me whole. I wasn't about to test the full limits of my immortality.

To my surprise, the basilisk whirled around and sent its long serpent's tail careening at me at a breakneck pace. I cursed and shot upward as quickly as I could, trying to escape it before it knocked me right out of the sky. I shot back tendrils of black smoke, trying to pin the thing in place, but it tore through them like they were nothing more than tissue paper. I cursed and dropped the magic, going back to flinging balls of hellfire at it as I gradually drew it farther away from its cave. It was very reluctant to leave, not taking more than a couple of steps forward at a time, until I finally gave up and started getting in close enough for the basilisk to actually catch me.

It was stupid, but we were running out of time. I needed to be able to get Eira in that cave before it noticed her. She would only wait, blindfolded and in her wolf form, for so long. The longer we took, the more likely the basilisk would smell or hear her, and I didn't want her to try and fight it.

I landed on the ground some distance away, staring at the beast as I planned my next move. Hellfire should have torn it to shreds, but its skin must have been made of some pretty tough stuff. I wished I'd brought Lucifer's sword,

Morningstar, with me, but even that might not have done anything to the basilisk. I was meant to fight demons and angels, as was the sword, not ancient creatures of legend.

I roused my undead army, or what was left of them, and had them charge forward to fight the basilisk again. If I could get close enough to the beast to touch it, I might be able to drain some of its life. I watched as the basilisk lashed out at my army with enormous claws, each the size of my entire arm. I definitely didn't want to find out how much they hurt.

I finally called my horse, Ghost, not knowing what else to do. He appeared at my side, looking less than pleased, and tossed his pale head. The basilisk let out a shriek, as if it had finally found a worthy opponent, and took a few steps forward. The horse simply blinked once at me with its glowing purple eyes, and then turned and pawed at the ground.

The basilisk slid out farther, its tail finally leaving an opening large enough for a white wolf to slip in. I looked around, trying to see if I could catch sight of Eira, but she'd done an excellent job of camouflaging herself and I had no idea where she was. I could only hope she'd be ready to go when the time was right.

I lit my hands with hellfire as Ghost continued staring the basilisk down, as if to say *bring it on*. My horse whickered once, and then we both charged at the beast. I ducked to one side, and the horse darted to the other, and the basilisk slid the rest of the way out of the cave in its attempt to come after us both.

Now! I thought at Eira, even though she couldn't hear me. Then I saw the flash of white fur as she darted into the cave, and I let out a sigh of relief. Of course, she also had to get out of the cave too, which meant my job here was just beginning.

I hopped on the back of Ghost, forming a sword made of shadow and hellfire, and charged the basilisk once more.

15

EIRA

The heat was almost oppressive in the cave. I had to open my mouth to pant to avoid overheating instantly, but at least it was a dry heat, not the moist, gross heat that was usually in dark, enclosed spaces like this.

I swiveled my ears around in lieu of my eyes, and flared my nostrils to catch the scents around me as I crept forward silently. The air smelled of death and sulfur, so strong it almost made me gag, and almost making me wish I'd done this as a human instead. Moving through the cave like this was difficult, but I managed to keep going, sticking close to the walls so I didn't lose my way.

As I continued forward, I caught scent of a huge pile of bones right in the middle of my path. I skirted it carefully, my flank brushing along the cave wall. I shuddered to think about what might be on that wall that was now on me, but I'd have to worry about getting clean later.

Outside, I heard the distant sounds of battle and hoped

Belial was all right, especially when a particularly loud roar echoed through the cave. I had to move quickly to get the Void key to avoid either of us getting hurt. Wait. When had I started caring so much about that bastard? Dammit, I'd told myself this morning that I would avoid him as much as possible, get the job done, and then never see him again. But now all I could think about was making sure he, the unkillable Death, was okay, when I should really be more worried about myself.

I kept creeping through the dark, hot cavern, though my heart was in my throat the whole time. I just wanted this to be over already, so we could stop the Furies and save the shifters and imps they'd brainwashed, including my brothers. Why couldn't Loki have hidden the key somewhere a little more accessible? He'd told me it was way in the back within the largest cavern, under a loose rock. I wasn't looking forward to trying to find it blindfolded.

Finally, the quality of sound changed, and the air seemed to be a little less oppressive, and I realized I must have reached the large cavern. Loki had said it would be on the right side, and that I would find it about halfway back. Which really wasn't all that much help.

Please be here, I thought as I stuck close to the wall and kept going.

A sudden noise behind me made me freeze. I swiveled my head around, trying to catch the source of the sound. The smell of sulfur intensified instantly, and every hair on my body rose straight up. I still didn't know exactly what it was, but it was bad and my instincts were screaming at me to run. I had barely enough time to throw up an ice shield around myself as something hissed through the air.

Fire impacted against my ice shield and sizzled. I balked at the sudden rush of heat, almost too much to take. Who the fuck was throwing fireballs at me?

My shield crumbled as a horrible screech echoed through the chamber, and then something started stomping toward me. It sounded very similar to the thing outside that Belial was fighting, but from the sound of its movements, it was a lot smaller.

A baby basilisk!

Fuck, this was bad. I wanted to run with every fiber of my being, but I couldn't leave until I had the Void key. It had to be here somewhere. I scrambled at the wall with my paws in a desperate frenzy, trying to find the loose rock Loki had told me about, while also trying to keep an ear or two on the basilisk as it drew closer. The thing was moving slowly, like it wasn't sure it should attack me again, or perhaps it was waiting for its parent to come help finish me off. Either way, I created another ice shield around me, making it as big as I could and praying it would hold. Then I felt something shift. A loose rock.

I pushed it aside, but there were lots of rocks below it, and I couldn't tell if I'd found the Void key or not. I didn't have time trying to test every single rock either, not when the basilisk kept approaching. With quick movements, I nudged the blindfold aside with one paw and looked down at the space I'd opened up.

There, amidst the rubble and the dull stones of the cave,

was a gemstone that looked very similar to my key to Faerie. It was small, round, and polished, but instead of being filled with a myriad of colors, it was a deep black with stars and mist in it.

I quickly grabbed it in my mouth, making sure to only look down at the ground in front of me. I spotted the shadow of the baby basilisk creeping closer behind me, like something out of a nightmare, and I quickly slipped my blindfold back down to protect my eyes.

Then I backed up, trying to find a way out of the cave without using my eyes, while also somehow getting past the baby basilisk that wanted to eat me for breakfast. The thing suddenly charged me, and I let loose a stream of icy shards at it, which made it pause long enough for me to put a little more distance between us. It unleashed more fire on me and began melting my ice shield, which wasn't meant to withstand this kind of power. Fighting this thing would be useless. I had to run for it.

I released a huge blast of ice toward what I thought was its face, trying to knock the thing back. It didn't work, but the creature let out a terrible screech, that sounded almost like a chicken's squawk. My back bumped into a wall, and I spun around to book it out of there, racing on my wolf's legs, but heard the damn basilisk coming after me.

I stumbled and fell over a rock in my path as I tried desperately to outrun the baby basilisk, but it was gaining fast on me. I held my breath as I rounded the pile of bones that meant that I was almost to the cave entrance, and I started running as fast as my four legs would allow. Finally, the basilisk, which had been gaining on me to the point of almost catching up, fell behind.

A slight flicker of hope broke through my terror me as the light from the outside of the cave filtered in through the tightly woven fabric of my blindfold. *Almost there... almost...* I burst into the light and started sprinting toward the cover of the trees nearby, briefly noting the smells of death, sulfur, horse, and Belial nearby. If I could just make it past the main part of the clearing and into the forest, I'd be safe. I hoped.

I'm going to make it, I thought, just before something huge and heavy plowed into me. A giant serpent's tail. It tossed me into the air several feet, and I let out a surprised cry and clenched down hard on the Void key as I went flying and landed awkwardly on my left side. Ow. That was definitely no baby basilisk. Somehow I'd gotten the attention of the mom. Or dad? I had no idea, and didn't really care, as pain lanced through me.

I scrambled up, trying to find my bearings, but then I was dragged down once again. Something sharp pricked at my thigh, and then set it on fire. I screamed at the feel of hot venom pulsing through my veins and heard Belial shouting as well. Some instinct made me shift back into human form, and the change in my size let me slip out of the basilisk's grasp, though I could do little more than scramble away on my hands and feet while unbearable pain spread through my body. The Void key had fallen from my mouth somewhere along the way, and I reached around until I found it, clasping it tight in my hand. The blindfold slipped off of my face and I shut my eyes tight, not willing to risk meeting the gaze of either basilisk.

Pure adrenaline shot me forward, and I stumbled the rest of the way to the edge of the forest, fighting through the agony. The baby basilisk was hot on my heels, so close that I could hear its clawed feet hitting the ground and feel the reverberation run up my own legs. I screamed again as I launched myself forward, and then turned around and blasted the baby basilisk with as much ice as I could call at once.

It was too much. The venom was already taking root in my system and making me weak, and then using so much power finally did me in. I collapsed and waited for the end.

But it didn't come.

Belial let out a roar that sounded less human than anything I'd heard from him yet, and then he landed next to me only seconds later. I heard the sizzle of him flinging hellfire, in such large amounts that I was surprised the forest around us wasn't already ablaze.

"I got the key," I muttered, unable to move. "Take it and go."

"Hold onto it. We're getting out of here."

He swooped me up into his strong arms, and I let out a sigh as I sank against him, finding comfort in his nearness. His large wings flapped, and then I felt the dizzying sensation of being lifted into the air at a speed so fast it took my breath away. I clutched the Void key tightly with one hand and gripped Belial's shirt with the other, deliriously trying to hold on as tightly as I could while he flew us away from the basilisks. Finally, I opened my eyes to watch the forest whizzing by beneath us and instantly regretted it as nausea made me gag.

After some time, which might have been minutes and might have been days, Belial slowed and started descending. We landed on the ground, and when I tried to put weight on my leg again, I let out a cry. The venom was acting fast, and I had no idea how long I'd be able to hang on. Belial watched me, his eyes dark and furious, but before he could say anything, his purple-eyed horse appeared out of nowhere.

"Ghost can run a lot faster than I can fly," Belial explained as he helped me onto the back of the horse, who tossed his head in annoyance.

"Where are we going?" I asked, my voice more like a frog's croak. I slumped forward on the horse's neck, unable to summon the strength to hold myself up.

"To get you help." Belial climbed on behind me, wrapping his arms around me, pulling me back against his hard chest in an almost protective manner. "I won't let you die."

"That's ironic, considering you're Death," I said with a delirious laugh, before everything went black.

16

EIRA

I opened my eyes to vibrant purple flowers creeping along a trellis above me, with a crystal clear blue sky behind it. The colors were so intense that I had to close my eyes again to stop them from tearing up. The sound of birds chirping and a bubbling stream met my ears. Everything smelled like flowers and a perfect breeze teased along my skin. It was so peaceful and idyllic, I wondered if this was a dream.

"You're awake."

My eyes flew open and I turned to face the sound of a melodious deep voice. A gorgeous fae male moved toward me, wearing a crown of ivy above his pointed ears. He wore a breezy white shirt that showed off his muscular chest, above black trousers that looked like silk. His hair appeared black at first, until the sunlight glinted off it, and I saw it was actually dark, luxurious blue. I blinked at him a few times, trying to figure out who he was. Something about him was familiar, but the shape of his face wasn't quite fully fae—it was a little too rugged and masculine. He must have been half fae, like me. The other half? I had no idea.

"Shit, I better not be at the Summer Court," I muttered before I could stop myself.

He laughed, and the sound was beautiful too. "No, this is the Spring Court, darling." He gave me a flirtatious wink. "Don't worry, you're perfectly safe here. I'll make sure of that."

Everything about him was charming, and it might have been endearing, if I hadn't woken up in this strange place and couldn't remember how I'd gotten here. "The Spring Court?" I asked, frowning as his words finally made sense.

His gaze swept across my body, though more in a concerned way this time. "How are you feeling?"

"Um. I don't really know." I tried to move, but everything felt sluggish. I also noticed I wasn't wearing my combat leathers anymore, but a breezy green dress covered in tiny purple flowers. "Nothing hurts, at least, but what happened to my clothes?"

"They were destroyed by the basilisk's venom. To save your life, Belial and I had to tear them off you."

My cheeks flashed with heat, knowing I'd been naked in front of the men, and that one or both of them had put me in this dress. "And then you dressed me."

"Don't worry, we were careful to preserve your modesty the entire time. Although you must know you are very beautiful, even when you're on the verge of death."

His hand reached toward my face, as if to brush away a piece of hair in my eyes, but before he could make contact, Belial stepped into my line of vision and knocked the fae's hand away. "Don't fucking touch her, Damien."

Damien just laughed and stepped back. "Wow, you really are possessive over her."

Belial shoved Damien away, and leaned over me himself. He ran his hands over my arms and tilted my head side to side, looking me over with a frown. Finally, he moved down to my leg, and I remembered. Ah, yes, the basilisks. What a fun time that had been. I grimaced at the memory, and wondered how I survived.

"I'm fine," I said, shrugging away Belial's hands from my body. I was a little groggy, but there was no pain. "Can you help me sit up?"

Belial helped me sit up, while my head spun a bit and then settled into normalcy. I looked down at my leg, but couldn't see a single trace of the wound that I'd sustained from the basilisk. It felt a lot better, with not even a twinge of pain as I moved it. When I clenched my hand reflexively, I realized that somehow I'd managed to keep hold of the Void key. I stared at it for a few moments, and then glanced up to find both Damien and Belial watching me.

"What happened?" I asked. "How did we get here?"

"I raced as fast as I could to the only place in Faerie that I knew could help you," Belial said. "Damien has a healing gift, especially good for poisons...and alcohol. It was particularly useful when he was in his Dionysus days as the god of wine."

"And orgies," Damien chimed in with a wicked grin.

Oh shit. I'd heard tales of the Spring Court palace. Which meant that the person standing in front of me had to be the Spring Court prince. I should have known immediately from the name and the crown on his head, but my brain was still catching up to all of this.

"You're safe here," Damien added as he noted my uncomfortable look. "No one will dare harm my brother's lady."

"Brother?" I asked, looking between the two men. That must be why Damien looked so familiar. He was Lucifer's son too.

Damien flashed me another flirty smile. "Yes, I'm Belial's younger, better looking, and far more charming brother."

Belial growled at that, and Damien shot me a look as if to say, *he's proving my point, isn't he?*

I hid a smile behind my hand. I liked Damien immediately. "Thank you for saving me."

"Thank Belial," Damien said with a knowing look in his eyes. "He somehow kept you alive on the journey here, which should have been impossible."

I frowned at Belial and opened my mouth to ask him what he'd done, but he shook his head.

"Now that you're better, we should get you back to Earth," he said.

"Please, stay the night," Damien said. "Or at least for dinner. Let Eira regain some of her strength. Demeter should be back by then too."

"Just one more reason to leave now," Belial grumbled. "She doesn't like me."

"No one does," Damien said, but he laughed right after, and Belial only rolled his eyes a little bit instead of threatening to kill him on the spot, so I figured it was a joke.

My brain was still a bit groggy, but even I realized they were talking about the Spring Queen—Damien's grandmother. I'd never met her, but I'd heard she could be...prickly. I didn't really feel up to being sociable at the moment though, especially with royalty. "I feel fine. I'd like to head back to Earth sooner than later."

Damien nodded. "Very well, if the lady insists. I can open a portal for you whenever you're ready."

"We're ready," Belial said, his voice leaving no room for argument. I got the sense he didn't want to be here a second longer than needed either.

"Of course." Damien clasped him on the shoulder, his face softening. "But I mean it, brother. You and your woman are always welcome here, even when you don't need anything. It would be nice to see you more than once every few decades."

"I'm not his woman," I said quickly.

Damien laughed. "That's not true and you know it."

Belial scowled. "Fine, I'll try to visit more often, but first we need to take care of a problem back in New Orleans."

"Whatever it is, I'm sure you'll be able to solve it," Damien said. "I'll open a portal back to your place now."

He stepped back so Belial could help me get to my feet. I let him lift me, and then pushed him away. I'd already been weak enough around him, and I needed to make sure he didn't think I needed to rely on him completely. I regretted it instantly when I swayed on my feet, but eventually I regained my balance. My supernatural healing was taking over now that the poison had left my body, and every second that passed made me feel a little stronger.

"You shouldn't be walking yet," Belial said, and before I could protest, he picked me up like I was a bride and he was about to carry me over the threshold.

"I can walk," I snapped. "Put me down." I didn't want Belial's brother to think I was some helpless woman who needed to be carted around like an invalid, but Belial just ignored me. Stubborn ass!

"See? So possessive." Damien chuckled as he reached into his pocket. He pulled out his own Faerie key and held it out, opening the swirling, colorful portal before us.

Belial started toward the portal but then paused and turned back to Damien. "You know, you can come and visit me as well. I'm only a portal away."

"I would, but every time I return to Earth, my visit somehow turns into a wine-filled orgy." Damien winked at me as he said it.

"Keep your dick in your pants and you'll be fine," Belial said, rolling his eyes. "Although I do have a great wine collection at my bar."

Damien grinned again. "All right, you've convinced me. I'll try to come visit you more too."

Belial nodded and carried me forward toward the portal. I'd given up resisting at this point, my body too weak to fight him off properly, even if this was humiliating. And kind of nice, at the same time, though I would never admit that out loud.

"Thank you again," he said to Damien, and then we stepped through the portal.

We arrived outside, in the alley behind Belial's building, and compared to Faerie, everything here seemed suddenly a lot dimmer. Belial immediately started toward the door, with me still clutched in his hands.

"Are you seriously going to carry me all the way up to your place?" I said, straining to get away from him. "Put me down."

"No, you need to save your strength."

"Maybe we should have stayed for dinner then," I said, slapping at his chest ineffectively when trying to wriggle out of his grasp didn't work. "Then I could have regained it."

Belial only grunted, and didn't give me an answer as he carried me up the stairs to his apartment. He entered the key code and kicked the door open, then stomped inside. He carried me all the way into his bedroom and deposited me onto his bed.

I sat up on the edge of it and glared at him. "You're fucking ridiculous. I'm not some damsel in distress."

"You're a damsel," Belial countered. "And you were in distress."

Fury washed up inside of me, and I threw an ice blast at him. I knew it wouldn't do anything more than annoy him, and he knocked it aside easily.

"Still trying to kill me even after I saved your life?" he

asked, arching an eyebrow. "You know by now that won't work."

"No, but this will." I stood up and held the Void key to his neck. "I can use this on you."

Belial took a step closer, until we were basically on top of each other, as he stared into my eyes with a challenge. "You won't."

"What's stopping me?" I asked, suddenly breathless.

"This."

Belial's hands slid into my hair, and then his mouth crashed down on mine. Shock washed through me as he kissed me hard, followed by a rush of desire and a sense of *rightness*. I dropped the Void key almost instantly, my hands needing to touch him instead, to wrap around his neck and pull him even closer. His kiss seemed to melt the ice around my heart, and I couldn't get enough of it. I demanded more of his lips, his tongue, his taste. He groaned in response and devoured me with the same primal need, and something within me shifted. Like I'd had this aching, empty feeling inside me all along, but now someone had taken a cup and poured in Belial, filling me up for the first time ever.

We belong together, I realized, and then wondered what the fuck would have brought that thought on. Then it struck me, and I pulled back with a gasp, looking at Belial's face for any indication of whether he felt it too. His eyes flashed with possessive need, like he was ready to pull me back into his arms again, and my soul sang for him to do it. It was clear he'd been struck by the same madness.

Surely, it couldn't be—a mate bond? No. It wasn't possible. I wouldn't accept it. But it felt so damn *right*.

How could Death, the killer of my father, be my fated mate?

Belial reached for me again and lust ran through me, answering his call, and I wanted nothing more than for him to rip off my clothes and claim me completely. But somehow I managed to back away, stepping out of range, still trembling with the revelation of what we were to each other.

"No," I said, shaking my head. "You can't be my fated mate."

"I am," Belial said, gazing at me with absolute certainty. "I didn't believe it at first either, but it explains the pull between us. Now the kiss has confirmed it."

"I don't believe it." I covered my face with my hands, trying to block him out, even though he was now a part of me I couldn't ignore. The kiss had activated the mate bond fully, and I knew, deep down, things would never go back to the way they were before. Fuck.

"It's how I was able to keep you alive," Belial said. "I

shared some of my power with you and it brought you back from the dead."

I dropped my hands and gaped at him. "No. That's impossible."

"It's the truth. The sooner you accept that we're mates, the easier it will be on both of us."

I sank back down on the bed, feeling suddenly weak again. "How is this even possible? This has to be a mistake."

Belial watched me for a moment, and then opened up his closet and shoved his clothes aside, revealing a huge safe in the back. I'd seen it during my time snooping around the apartment, but obviously couldn't open it. He entered a code and the door swung open, and then he removed a huge, sheathed sword from inside. Okay, that was not what I'd expected to be in there.

"Take this," he said, holding it out to me hilt-first.

I stared up at him, trying to figure out why he was giving this to me, but his eyes were impassive. I gingerly wrapped my hand around the hilt. "Why?"

"This is Morningstar, an ancient sword forged specifically for Lucifer, and him alone. It burns anyone else who touches it."

"It's not burning me."

"Only Lucifer, his fated mate, and their children can hold it..." Belial paused, arching his eyebrows at me. "And their mates."

I quickly thrust the sword back at him. "And if I refuse?"

His mouth curved up in a smirk. "We both know you won't."

"I could reject you, you know. It's been done before."

"Impossible." Belial's eyes flashed with dark fire. "Now that I've confirmed you're my mate, I'm not letting you go."

A shiver ran through me at his possessive words, and I hated how much I liked them. I crossed my arms. "I don't want this."

"I wasn't looking for this either, but there's no way we can deny it." He set the sword down and took a step closer to me, like he couldn't fight the pull between us any longer. "Besides, I need you."

I clenched my hands into fists at the vulnerable note in his voice. *Don't get taken in by it,* I told myself sternly. "What are you talking about?"

He breathed in sharply, then sat on the bed beside me. "To become Death, I had to sacrifice my soul. I've been hollow ever since, like I'm missing a part of myself." He paused and his face tightened, almost as if he was in pain. "And then there's the hunger."

"Hunger?" I asked.

"The hunger for death. I have to steal life to sate it, or I'll lose control." He slanted a dark look at me. "That would be very dangerous for everyone."

My throat tightened. "Is that why you go hunting every night?"

He nodded. "If I have to kill, I can at least try to protect my city at the same time. But when I met you, everything changed. The hunger fades away when you're near. Every time we touch, I feel complete again."

"What does that mean?" I asked.

His hand cupped my cheek. "It means you're my mate. I've lived for thousands of years and even though I had another mate once before, I've never felt anything like this. I assumed I would never find love again, especially once I gave up my soul. But then I met you."

"Belial..." I swallowed hard, as I found myself leaning into his touch. "None of this makes any sense."

"You're my other half. There's no denying it."

This time when he pulled me into his arms and kissed me, I gave in. I pressed myself against him, letting his words echo through my head. I could *feel* the truth of them, and the mate bond was impossible to deny, no matter how much I wanted to fight it. All we could do was let it sweep us away.

The kiss between us grew more intense, and I trembled as Belial ran his hands over my body, tracing my curves through my thin Spring Court dress. When he captured my breast in his palm and gave a light squeeze, I gasped against his lips. My fingers tangled in his dark hair, needing to touch him, to keep his mouth on me for as long as I could. Kissing him was like being ravished, and I couldn't get enough.

His broke the kiss to my dismay, but then he trailed his lips down my neck, and I sighed and arched to give him better access. His mouth sent heat through me with every kiss, while his thumbs traced my nipples, making them hard as pebbles. Then his hands skimmed down my body, to my hips, and then to my thighs, where he fisted the fabric of my dress and pulled it higher. And higher. Giving him access to the soft skin of my thighs, and everything between them.

"Are you wet for me, my mate?" he asked, his voice low in my ear. "Let's find out."

His large fingers slipped between my thighs, and I realized the men hadn't bothered to put underwear on me when they'd dressed me. Typical. I couldn't complain though, not when Belial traced a finger over the folds of my pussy with a satisfied smirk.

"Mmm, very wet indeed."

His finger suddenly plunged inside me, making me gasp. My hands tightened around his tattooed arms, not to stop him, but to stop myself from falling over. I was still a bit tired from what had happened, but more than that, I was overwhelmed by what he was making me feel. Then he pulled his finger out and slid it into his mouth, tasting me, while his eyes locked on mine. Inside them I saw that hunger he spoke of, though I could see that he craved me and not death. The intensity of his desire made me weak in the knees, and I knew I wouldn't be able to resist him. Nor did I really want to anymore.

"You taste even better than I imagined," he said. "But I need more."

He fell to his knees in front of me and pressed his nose into the gap between my thighs, shoving the dress up even higher. I gasped as his face nuzzled against me and I gripped his shoulders, anxiously awaiting whatever he would do next. Anticipation mixed with desire and set my body alight. I could hardly hear anything over the sound of my beating heart.

Finally, he dipped his mouth between my thighs and

found my clit. I let out a moan as he explored my pussy, taking his sweet time, like he wanted to devour every inch of me. My head fell back as he teased me with his tongue, licking and sucking, but never quite giving me enough to set me over the edge. His hands gripped my hips, holding me in place, and each tightening of his fingers against my skin sent little shocks of pleasure though me. Every muscle in my body was clenched tight, waiting for more.

Belial yanked my hips to the edge of the bed and began devouring me like I was is favorite meal. I dug my hands into his still-clothed shoulders, my claws shredding the material of his shirt like it was nothing. Belial didn't do anything but growl and double down, almost as if he was egging me into an orgasm, pushing me closer and closer to the edge of it. I leaned my head back, waves of pleasure running through me, as it built and built. Finally it was too much and I came with a shout, my legs trembling, my hands hanging onto Belial's shoulders like I might be lost if I let go.

"You taste divine," he said, licking his lips, and my already weak legs threatened to give out completely at that. He rose to his feet and began pulling off his shirt, drawing my eyes to his chest. I sucked in a breath as his skin was revealed before me, every perfect inch of his muscled body. He reached for his jeans next.

"Belial..." I said, making him pause. He probably thought I was going to push him away or end this now. Instead I looked up at him with everything I wanted clear in my eyes and said, "Don't stop."

"I don't intend to." With a carnal grin, he slid his jeans

down, along with whatever was underneath. I'd had a glimpse of his impressive cock before, but hadn't allowed myself to really look at it. Now I gave myself permission to stare, and I drank in the sight of it—long, thick, and hard, and all for me.

Then he gripped the light fabric of my dress in his fists again, and lifted the entire thing above my head. I wore nothing underneath and his gaze roamed over me, taking me in while the hunger in his eyes only grew more intense.

"I've lived for thousands of years, but you're the most beautiful thing I've ever seen," he said, and my heart skipped a beat at the words. Then his voice dipped lower. "And now I shall claim you as mine."

He pushed me down on the bed, his hands almost rough, though I knew he would never truly hurt me. With desperate need, he yanked my legs apart and settled between them, like he couldn't wait even a second longer. Then his eyes met mine as his cock thrust into me, hard and fast. I let out a soft cry as he filled me completely and wrapped my legs around him, bringing him closer to me and pulling him in deeper.

Something clicked into place as he bottomed out, as if I'd been missing this my entire life, and now I was finally whole. I met his gaze as he began moving inside me, shocked at the feeling of how right it felt.

He's my mate.

I finally accepted it, unable to deny the bond between us any longer. Somehow fate had brought us together, and I knew it was never letting us go after this. Our lives were bound together forever from this moment onward. The thought of that still scared me, but it was hard to worry about it when Belial's cock was pounding into me, sending unimaginable pleasure through my entire body.

I wrapped my arms around him, trying to bring him closer, to pull him deeper. I wanted to feel him at the very core of me, deep in my soul. Belial let out a low growl, as if he felt the same need, and he yanked up my hips, trying to fill me even more. The friction against my clit at this angle, along with the slide of his cock in and out of me, had me whimpering. I was hardly off of my first orgasm, and he was already hurtling me toward a second.

"You're mine," he growled, but then he suddenly rolled us over, so I was on top, straddling him. "But I'm yours too."

"Mine..." I whispered, gazing down at him, feeling his cock pulsing inside me. The word felt strange on my lips. How had Belial gone from being an enemy to being *mine*?

"Show me," he ordered. "Ride me. Fuck me. *Claim* me."

I drew in a breath and pressed my hands to his chest, then began moving up and down on him. Slowly at first. It was easier to let him claim me. To be his. But I wanted him to me mine too. Desperately. And maybe he needed to see that.

With each rock of my hips, my pace increased, as did the pleasure. He dug his fingers into my hips and thrust upward to meet me, and soon I was riding him fast and hard, chasing my own pleasure, needing to feel that cock deeper and deeper inside me. I threw my head back and let go, and then my vision whited out and I clenched around him, spinning into another orgasm, this one even more intense than the first.

I cried his name as I rode him through my orgasm, and he groaned and thrust up harder in response as his own climax swept over him. I didn't want it to end though, so I kept going, until we were both so spent that he wrapped his arms around me and dragged me down against his chest, his cock still throbbing inside me.

Aftershocks of pleasure went through me as the mate bond sealed. It was done. I was bonded to Belial, and we would be mates forever now. Before I might have resisted it, but now I closed my eyes and gave in to the feeling. I wanted it, more than I'd ever wanted anything in my life.

I didn't know what would happen between us, or how we could ever truly be together, but for the first time in my life I finally felt like I belonged.

18

EIRA

I opened my eyes to a dark room and immediately knew I was alone. Belial's scent lingered in the air, but I didn't hear his movements anywhere in the apartment. The sleek, modern alarm clock on his bedside table told me it was 2 AM. I hadn't even remembered falling asleep, but then again, Belial had thoroughly worn me out last night, and I'd already been pretty tired from the whole nearly-dying thing. Good thing I healed fast.

I glanced over at Belial's side of the bed, even though I knew he wouldn't be there. Where had he gone? Down to his bar? Or on another one of his nightly hunts? He'd told me he had to kill to keep the hunger for death under control, but he'd also said that being around me calmed that need. Yet now he was gone again, and I didn't know what to think. Maybe killing was now a compulsion for him, an addiction he couldn't get over, no matter what he said. Why else would he leave me so soon after we'd just sealed our mate bond?

"What have I done?" I whispered, as regret and shame washed over me. I'd come to New Orleans to kill Belial, not sleep with him. *Definitely* not to become his mate. This was all wrong. But even now I couldn't stop wanting him. I pressed the palms of my hands into my eyes, as if I could forget every earth-shattering orgasm I'd had at his hands, and lips, and cock...

Stop it! I told myself. I sucked in a breath and tried to pull myself together. I needed to get out of this place so I could think without all of the reminders of Belial—and his absence—around me.

I ignored my discarded Spring Court dress on the floor and went for my luggage in the living room, where I pulled out a gray t-shirt and jeans. I'd go out and get some fresh air to clear my head, before coming back here, and Belial would probably never even know I was gone. And if he did know, why did I care? I wasn't his prisoner anymore. I could go where I wanted. If he had a problem with that, too fucking bad.

I left quickly, making my way down the stairs to the door into Belial's garage. His sleek Ducati motorcycle was parked beside his Aston Martin, and I debated which one I was going to borrow. I got on the bike and started it up, planning to ride around the city for a while with no real destination in mind. As I revved the motor, I considered going to Loki, but I wasn't ready to give him the Void key yet, and I had a feeling he wouldn't be amused by the news that I'd become

Belial's mate. The two of them seemed to have some bad blood between them.

As I rode out of the garage, something strange bubbled up inside me, yanking me in one direction. It had been a few days since I'd last felt it—the call of the Furies.

I tried to ignore it, gritting my teeth and driving faster. I wasn't going to be under anyone's control. Not Belial's, and not the Furies' either. But the more I tried to deny the pull, the stronger it got, and somehow I looked up and found myself staring at the rusted, faded sign outside Jazzland. I didn't even remember the journey, like my body had taken over even while my mind fought back.

I got off the bike, wondering why they'd brought me here now. The abandoned amusement park was even more eerie at night, just like when I'd dreamed about it, and my skin crawled even as the tug in my gut made me take steps forward.

But as soon as I climbed over the fence and entered the desolate place, I got the feeling I was alone. I breathed in sharply, able to use my wolf senses now that I no longer wore the cuffs, but didn't smell any shifters or imps around me. The few lingering scents were a few days old, as if they'd cleared out of the place just after Belial and I had found them. But where had they gone? And why was I still drawn to this place?

The sound of quiet steps on the sidewalk made me freeze. Something flickered in the corner of my eye, and I jerked my head toward it. I raised my fists, ready to call on my ice magic to defend myself, but relaxed a tiny bit as I smelled my brother's familiar scent.

Skoll was in wolf form as he approached, his black fur blending into the night, but his burning red eyes gave away his position. Another sound on the other side of me caught my attention, along with a second familiar scent. I spun around as my other brother, Hati, crept toward me, his white fur bristling.

I glanced between both of them nervously as they approached, while tension hung between us. I'd never been afraid of them before in my life, but now I wasn't sure if they were truly themselves anymore.

When they made no move to attack me, I asked, "Where did the Furies go?"

"They prepare to bring Tisiphone to Earth tonight, at the Blood Moon," Skoll said.

That must be the name of the Fury of vengeance. "How?"

"Sacrifice," Hati growled.

That didn't sound good. "What kind of sacrifice?"

Hati bared his fangs in a dark, dangerous smile. "You'll see."

"Join us," Skoll said, as they prowled around me in a circle. "Together we can stop Belial. With the Furies, even he won't be able to stand against our might and power."

"Belial isn't the enemy," I said. "The Furies are."

"He's in her head," Hati growled.

Skoll's red eyes narrowed. "Eira, have you forgotten that he killed our father? Along with many other shifters?"

"I haven't forgotten, but you never told me the whole story. Like how Dad became Death, the fourth Horseman, and lost himself completely."

"Does it matter?" Skoll asked, his ears twitching. "None of that changes that Belial was the one to end his life."

"He needs to be stopped before he kills more of our people," Hati added.

I bit my lip, torn between my brothers and my mate. I understood how my brothers felt, because I'd shared the same feelings only days ago, when rage and a need for vengeance had consumed me. Besides, Belial could be out there right now, killing at this very moment, and I wasn't sure I would be able to ever stop him.

But I couldn't kill Belial either. He was my mate, no matter how much I'd tried to deny it, and we were bound together for the rest of our immortal days. I wasn't ready to admit that to my brothers just yet though. I could only imagine the way their rage would turn upon me if they knew.

I had to be careful here. My brothers were still being controlled by the Furies, and picking Belial over them could lead to my death. Besides, if I could convince them I was their ally, they might give me information, which I could use to stop the Furies tonight.

"You're right," I said. "He has to be stopped. I will join you."

"To join us, you must betray him," Skoll said, cocking his wolf head. "Can you do this?"

"Yes," I lied. "It won't be a problem."

Hati gave a sly, cold smile. "Good. Welcome back to the pack."

"Bring Belial to the Ursuline Convent at midnight," Skoll said. "We will deal with him then."

I nodded, feeling a lump in my throat. "We'll be there."

"And vengeance will finally be ours," Hati said.

They slipped away into the shadows and I drew in a deep breath, relieved to be alone again, even if this place gave me the creeps. I ducked my head and rubbed my arms against the chill in them, which had nothing to do with the weather, as I set off for the bike again.

A movement in the sky caught my attention and I looked up, not sure what to expect this time. Belial swooped down on his beautiful black and white ombre wings, his long cape flowing behind him. As he drew close, the cold look on his face could have killed on the spot. He truly looked like Death at that moment—and he was coming right for me.

But I wasn't afraid. I stood my ground, waiting for him to land, refusing to run away. I knew he would never hurt me.

"What are you doing here?" he growled, the second his feet touched the ground. "Why did you leave?"

"I could ask you the same thing," I said, glaring back at him. "I woke up and you were gone."

He raised his eyes to the sky. "I had something to deal with in the bar. I was coming right back."

"Well, how should I know that?" I asked. "I just needed to get away for a while, but then I found myself here."

His eyes narrowed and then he let out a low whistle and

his horse appeared. Belial's hands wrapped around my waist, and then he lifted me up like I weighed nothing and deposited me on Ghost's back. He climbed on behind me, wrapping his arms around me tightly, like he worried I might run away at any second.

"You're coming back with me," he said, as the horse took off running.

19

EIRA

A s Ghost raced forward alongside the highway, I
struggled against Belial, pushing his hand off of my
waist. Fury ignited inside me. He had no say over where I
went or what I did.

"I'll jump off of your damn horse," I threatened. "You
can't keep me like a pet."

"You're not my pet, you're my mate," Belial said, wrapping his arm around me once more. This time, he pinned my
arms flat against my sides, and it was impossible to break
free. "I'm not letting you go," he continued, his voice right in
my ear. I could feel his lips brushing the delicate shell of my
ear, and involuntary shivers went through me. "I lost my
mate once before, and it's never happening again."

I could hear real pain in his voice, and I softened. He'd
never spoken about this before, and though I was a little
jealous he'd had a mate before me, I was also intrigued.
"What happened?"

"She was a gargoyle named Soria and we were together for a century in Hell. But during my rebellion against my father, Loki betrayed us and she was killed."

"No wonder you hate him so much," I muttered.

"Indeed." His voice turned grim. "I lost the battle, I lost my lover, and I lost my family when I was exiled." The pain in his voice increased, and for the first time he sounded almost vulnerable. "I never thought I would ever find a mate again... Until now."

He tightened his hold against me more, but it felt reassuring rather than painful this time. I relaxed slightly against him. "Look, I don't know how or why we have this bond between us, but I'm not resisting it any longer. I wasn't running away. I just needed some space to think. Especially because I thought you had run away—or gone out hunting again."

"It seems we both overreacted a tiny bit," he admitted with a low chuckle. "The mate bond does tend to make one a little...crazy sometimes."

"So it seems."

"The feeling is stronger this time too." He nuzzled his lips against my neck. "I can't think of anything else but you."

"I know what you mean." My breath caught as his mouth brushed my skin and his hands tightened on my hips. Behind me, his cock pressed into my ass, hot and hard, and I couldn't help but squirm back into it. I wanted him inside me again, with a startling intensity.

"I think it's because I'm part fae," I gasped out as Belial's hand moved to cup my breast. "Our mating bonds are more intense than for demons and angels. The bond is almost all-consuming, especially at first. Or so I've heard."

"Yes, all-consuming..." He pinched my nipple while his teeth nipped at my neck. "I want to consume you right now."

I rocked back, trying to meet his cock, to get any kind of relief, and Belial let out a low growl. Ghost made an annoyed whine in response as his feet pounded against the pavement, while Belial's shadow magic concealed us from the few cars that drove along the highway at this hour.

Unable to stop myself, I reached back and slid my hand between our bodies, touching Belial through the fabric of his pants. He let out a harsh breath and rolled his hips into my body, then slid his free hand along the front of my jeans, dipping between my legs. He was talented with his fingers, even through the thick fabric, and he had me panting and moaning almost instantly.

I rubbed him through his pants, unable to get the leverage to properly take him in hand. Good thing the ride back to Belial's place was short. Ghost dropped us off with a disgusted snort, before disappearing into thin air.

Belial pushed me against the wall the moment we were inside of the building. I ran my hands over his chest, sliding my fingers under his shirt so I could feel the smooth, hard ridges of his abs.

"Should we go upstairs?" I asked.

"Do you want to wait that long?"

That was a fair point. I plunged my hand inside his pants and gripped his length. He let out a groan and thrust into my hand shallowly. I watched in wonder as his face opened, the last of the anger and hurt fading. It was replaced with pleasure, and when he looked at me, there was nothing but hunger in his eyes. He drew me closer and kissed me hard, the mate bond wrapping around us like a warm blanket, while he tugged open the front of my jeans. He slid them down without hesitation, taking my panties with them, just low enough for him to slide a finger into my wet pussy.

"Turn around," he commanded, and I did it without a second thought.

He moved behind me, pressing me against the wall, bringing his lips to the exposed skin of my neck. I heard him shove down his own pants and then felt his cock rubbing along my ass until it found the gap between my thighs.

I spread my legs wider and arched my back to give him better access. "Yes," I hissed as he slid his cock inside of me, my eyes fluttering shut.

Belial began slamming into me, hands on my hips to pull me back as he pleased. I put my hands flat on the wall, bracing myself against the impact. His pace was unrelenting, his body so strong it felt like he might tear me apart, but I welcomed it. I wanted it all.

It didn't matter how many times we did this, each time was just as good as the first one. There was something about the mate bond that made sex ten times better. I couldn't describe it, but it was like I was just now finding some hidden part of me that no one else had been able to touch.

I moaned as his cock hit me in just the right way, and then clamped my jaw shut, wondering if there was anyone around who could hear us. We were in the middle of the stairwell, where anyone could walk out and see us.

"Don't you dare be quiet," Belial growled. "I want to hear every noise you make for me. *Because* of me."

I squeezed my eyes shut as he found my clit with his fingers and began stroking it, while pounding into me again and again. Pretty soon I didn't have a choice but to let out little cries and moans as he claimed me with his cock. I wondered if people from the bar could hear me. *Do I even care?* I thought as my eyes rolled back in my head. *Not one bit.*

Then he suddenly pulled out and turned me around, plastering me up against the wall once more. "I want to see you when you come."

"Only if you come with me," I said, my voice breathless.

He growled at that as he wrapped my legs around his hips. I gasped as he entered me again, then reached forward and slid my hand around the back of his head, clutching at the nape of his neck. We stared into each other's eyes, turning this quick, desperate fuck into something so intimate it made my heart ache.

Overwhelming pleasure rocked through me like a lightning bolt and I screamed Belial's name, my pussy clenching around his cock. He continued slamming into me through my orgasm, but then he threw his head back and roared as his own release took hold of him. Then his mouth found mine again and we devoured each other, unable to get enough, even when he was still inside me.

Reluctantly, he let me go, and we yanked up our pants.

Then he lifted me in his arms and carried me up the stairs. This time, I didn't resist. Fuck, I wasn't sure if I could even make it up the stairs right now, after what he'd just done to me.

Once we returned to his living room, Belial set me down on the couch. "I'll make you something to eat."

"How did you know I was hungry?" I asked.

He grinned as he headed into the kitchen. "You're part shifter. As far as I can tell, they're always hungry."

I couldn't argue with that. I relaxed into the couch, trying to remember what I'd been doing before I'd been pinned against Belial's wall. Right, the Furies. "My brothers were there when I went to Jazzland again, but otherwise the place was empty."

"Did they say anything?" Belial asked, as he pulled out some bread and cheese.

"They're going to bring the third Fury into the world tonight, during the Blood Moon." I stood and went to stand beside him, setting my hand on his back as he worked, the mate bond demanding I touch him.

"How do they think they're going to do that?" he asked as he put the bread and cheese in the skillet, making a grilled cheese sandwich for me.

"They said something about a sacrifice, which can only be a bad thing. They told me to be at the Ursuline Convent tonight at midnight so I could join them."

Belial frowned at that as he grabbed a spatula. "The Ursuline Convent is one of the oldest structures in New Orleans. The nuns there used to care for the dying during the yellow fever outbreak and for wounded soldiers during the Civil War. It's seen a lot of death over the years. It's also where the famous Casket Girls lived."

"Casket Girls?" I asked, my eyebrows shooting up. "That sounds morbid."

"Not as morbid as you'd think," he said. "They were French women sent to be brides to men in New Orleans. They lived on the third floor of the convent, but a lot of people believed they'd brought evil in with them. Some also believed they were vampires."

"Well, with a name like that, I can see why," I muttered.

"They weren't vampires, of course, but even now, the Ursuline Convent is considered one of the most haunted places in the city because of all of the death that happened there."

"Do you believe in ghosts?" I asked, cocking my head at him. I'd never seen one, but maybe he had, since he was a lot older than me.

Belial shook his head. "I've seen a lot of strange shit in my life, but never a real ghost. Some creatures like to pretend, but they always end up being something else." He finished frying up the sandwich and put it on a plate for me. "Still, with its dark history, it's one of the places where the barrier between worlds is a little thinner, which is probably why they've chosen that spot. The Blood Moon will also make their magic more potent tonight."

"Makes sense," I said, before taking a bite of the sandwich, which was as simple as it was delicious. I had to admit,

I was enjoying being with a man who liked to keep me well-fed.

"Midnight, you said?" Belial asked, leaning back against the counter as he watched me eat.

"That's what they told me." I finished off the rest of the sandwich in record time.

"Then we'll be there tonight to stop whatever this sacrifice is, and we'll use our Void key to send the Furies back where they came from."

"Do you think that will be enough to free my brothers and the others the Furies have enthralled?"

"It should be. Once they're safely sealed back in Void, they won't have any power here anymore."

I nodded, but knew it wouldn't be easy. To stop the sacrifice and use the Void key, we'd have to go up against both my brothers and the Furies, along with all the other shifters and imps that followed them. Doing this would mean turning against my family completely, even though I was trying to help them. But in their eyes, I would be siding with Belial over them.

Choosing my mate over my family—could I really do it?

20

BELIAL

W ith the Blood Moon bright overhead, I carried Eira across New Orleans, keeping us wrapped in shadows so none would see us—although I suspected the Furies could sense my power as I approached. I sensed them too, like the presence of another Elder God or two was calling to me. With soft steps, I landed on the roof of the Ursuline Convent's main building, and pieces of it crumbled beneath me despite my caution. The white French colonial buildings below us were old, possibly the oldest structures left in New Orleans, and they formed a courtyard around a garden that looked almost like a maze.

I set Eira down and she nodded at me. She was dressed in all black, her white hair tied up in a bun, and my heart twisted at the sight of her. I'd do everything in my power to make sure she was safe tonight, but she was a warrior too—I would do her a disservice if I didn't allow her to fight.

With shadows concealing us, we walked to the edge of

the roof to peer down into the courtyard below. Dozens of shifters, imps, and even humans were gathered there, all facing the steps of the Convent, where the two Furies stood. They had their hands up and their eyes closed, and I heard a low, rhythmic chanting coming from their direction. On either side of them, acting as their guardians, were Eira's brothers, both in their wolf forms, one dark, and one light.

The crowd was all staring forward, completely entranced as the Furies continued chanting, and many of them appeared hostile. Their faces were twisted, their hands clenched into fists, their feet stomping almost comically.

"The Furies are spreading anger and jealousy," Eira whispered. She closed her eyes and shuddered slightly. "I can feel it."

"Will it be a problem?"

She breathed out slowly and met my eyes. "No. I can fight it."

I stared down at the people below, who seemed to grow more agitated by the second. "They're whipping these people into a frenzy. Soon things will get violent."

"We have to stop them," Eira said.

Before we could act, the Furies' chanting became louder, drowning out everything else, and then a wave of red and green magic passed over the assembled group. Without warning, the shifters and imps turned on the humans and began attacking them, ripping them apart like they were nothing more than animals, killing them with claws and talons and fangs within seconds.

Eira gasped at the horror of it all and clutched my arm. "This is the sacrifice."

"Yes." I'd seen countless battles during my life, but this was a bloodbath, and it happened so quickly it seemed impossible to stop. "And with every death, the Furies channel the power into creating a portal to Void."

As we watched, deathly power rippled back into the space between the two Furies, where the air shimmered like a heat mirage. Space and time were literally ripping open, and the veil between worlds was growing thinner with every human's death.

Eira took a step forward, nearly launching herself off the roof. "We have to do something before the portal is open!"

"It's too late," I said. "It's already open."

Eira looked over at me, her jaw clenched, her eyes burning with determination. "I have a plan. Can you distract the shifters and the imps so we can get down there?"

"Of course." I reached out with my Death magic, knowing it would alert the Furies, but we were past any subtlety now. I latched onto the dead humans in the courtyard and sent life back into them, or some semblance of it, anyway. It was always easier to raise the fresh dead, and they responded to my call immediately.

The shifters and imps began looking around in confusion as their recent kills started twitching, standing up, or crawling toward them. My undead shambled forward in a mass, going after the imps and shifters with their jerky, nightmarish movements, and then they began fighting against the very people who had just killed them.

"That should keep them busy for a while." I pulled Morningstar from the sheath I'd slung over my back and handed it to Eira. "Take this when you go. And be careful."

"I will." She stared down at the sword in awe as it lit up with black and white light, showing it was deadly to both angels and demons. Her own ice magic coated the blade too, as she tested the weight of it. "Thank you."

I grabbed her and kissed her soundly, trying to communicate everything I couldn't put into words with that kiss. Now that I'd found Eira and accepted who she was to me, I had a hard time letting her go, but we had a job to do here. No one else would be able to stop the Furies tonight except us.

"Don't die on me," I told her.

"I won't," she said with a mischievous grin. "After all, I have Death on my side."

I wrapped my arms around her and lifted off the roof, then dropped us down right in front of the Furies. Behind us was the throng of shifters and imps fighting their recent kills, but they didn't pay us any notice. Eira launched herself toward Alecto and Megaera, and I unleashed my own power against them, sending a flaming ball of hellfire at their dark, hooded forms. It crashed against them and they were buffeted backward, their chanting cut off immediately. The portal spasmed and began to grow thin, like mist that was being carried away by the night.

The Furies each unleashed an earsplitting scream of anger as they dragged themselves up and turned their full attention to me. Eira's brothers descended from the steps, their huge wolf forms almost as dangerous as the Furies. I prepared myself to fight them all, drawing upon my reserves of power. There might be a lot of them, but I was Death. I could not be defeated.

"Wait!" Eira's voice rang out across the din, cutting through it all. "Stop!"

Was this her plan? I readied my next hellfire shot, ready to protect her with everything I had, while I waited to see what she did next. Her brothers and the Furies paused though, almost as if they'd been expecting something like this.

"You don't need to kill any more people as a sacrifice," Eira said, holding her hands up in a placating gesture. "I have a Void key, and I'll use it to bring the third Fury to Earth."

What? I glanced her way, wondering if this was a trick. She wouldn't really give them the Void key, would she?

The Furies cocked their heads with dark smiles. "We knew you would see things our way," Alecto said.

"The only thing I ask for is the power of vengeance from the third Fury to send Belial into Void," Eira continued in a cool, even tone, without looking at me once.

The world seemed to disappear under my feet, dragging me down with it. Or at least that's how it felt, hearing Eira's words. Shock rippled through me at her betrayal, and I could only stare at her, wondering if I'd had it all wrong.

The two wolves seemed to grin at her words, their eyes burning with hatred as they fixated on me. Had they gotten to her when she'd met with them?

Or had she been plotting this all along and I'd been too infatuated by her to notice?

"Vengeance will be yours," Megaera said, gesturing for Eira to step forward. "Give us the Void key."

"Release the others first," Eira said, glancing back at the mad horde fighting behind us.

Alecto sighed as if this was a true hardship. "Very well."

Another wave of power erupted from them, and the shifters and imps behind us suddenly stumbled and collapsed. I reached out with a tiny bit of my power and found they were alive, just completely drained of energy. Their demon healing would kick in soon and they'd be fine, albeit somewhat traumatized. I couldn't say the same for the humans they'd killed though.

As Eira stepped toward the Furies, I called out, "Don't do this, Eira."

Her eyes finally locked onto mine, and all I saw in them was rage. "Stay away from me."

I staggered back under the weight of her hatred. She'd really turned against me. She must have been pretending to care about me all this time, gaining my trust so she could look for a way to defeat me, all the while plotting to betray me. Now she finally had her chance.

This can't be happening, I thought. *Turn around, look at me. Give me a sign that what we had was real.*

She didn't.

Her brothers dodged in front of me, blocking me from getting to her, as she clutched the Void key in her hand. I'd given up the fight at this point anyway. Why bother, when my own mate wanted me dead? Did any of this even matter, without her?

Another thought struck me, one that had festered inside of me ever since I'd become Death. Did I even deserve to live? Perhaps I belonged in Void with the other Elder Gods. The world would certainly be safer without me in it. Especially if I didn't have Eira at my side, calming my hunger.

Maybe this was the end of Death.

I held out the Void key and the portal burst open with a horrible ripping sound, like the world itself was being torn apart around me. A chaotic swirl of glittering lights and hazy mist formed against a black background that seemed as empty and vast as space. My eyes could barely comprehend the strange sights and the feeling of unknowable power in front of me, and I quickly turned my gaze away, fearing what would happen if I stared at the portal to Void too long.

Instead, I finally allowed myself to look back at Belial. I'd been avoiding it, afraid that everything would show on my face the moment I did. I didn't want the Furies to doubt me for a second, but now they weren't focused on me at all, but at the portal in front of me.

Belial stared at me, his face completely dead, with only defeat and heartbreak in his eyes. My heart wrenched in my chest, but before I could consider it further, there was an inhuman shriek, almost deafening in my ear.

I turned just in time to see a deathly yellow spirit full of rage pouring through the portal. The fury and need for vengeance hit me like a storm, and I doubled over. I coughed, as if it was something I needed to get out of my body physically, and then I heard one of the Furies speak.

"Sister, take Eira's body. She is your vessel!"

I'd known this was coming when I made my deal with the Furies, but panic still spiked inside me as the spirit surged toward me. As the Fury drew near, I was hit with the absolute need for revenge, the certainty that defeating Belial and having my vengeance was the most important thing in the world. All I had to do was let this Fury take over my body, and together we would be unstoppable.

"No!" Belial yelled.

A roar of bright blue hellfire went past my ear and slammed into the Fury of vengeance, who shrieked and fell back. It was just enough to break me of her spell and I shook my head, trying to clear it of her influence.

The other two Furies turned on Belial, and I watched as they changed. Alecto had possessed the body of a shifter, and now she changed into a giant alligator before my eyes. She let out a wild scream that faded into a roar, while Megaera grew the black talons of an imp, thanks to the body she possessed.

The huge, lumbering alligator lunged at Belial, who started aiming half of his hellfire balls at her. Meanwhile, Megaera slashed at him with her claws and then exploded into ten versions of herself with illusion magic, all circling around and diving at him. When my brothers joined in the fray, their wolves out for blood, I feared Belial wouldn't be able to withstand it all. He might not be able to die, but the Furies were slowly inching him toward the portal, making him lose ground to avoid getting caught by claws or a heavy sweep from the Fury's alligator tail. I had to do something to save him.

While Belial shot hellfire at the Furies, his undead army came up behind him, and they tackled my brothers. The wolves snapped and tore at the zombie-like human corpses, but there were too many of them. With a flick of his deathly power, Belial knocked both of the wolves out, my brothers collapsing into the grass. I hoped they were only knocked out anyway, and not dead.

Now it was only the three Furies fighting against Death. Four immortals, locked in a power struggle that would only end when some of them were shoved into Void.

Finally, I saw my opportunity. I unsheathed Morningstar and raced toward Megaera, the green-eyed Fury of jealousy who was using the imp's magic to confuse Belial. She took a few stumbling steps back as Belial hit her with hellfire square in the chest, and she didn't hear me coming up behind her. I was able to grab hold of her loose robe and pull her back onto Morningstar. She let out a wail, scrabbling at me and the sword, but I encased her in ice, her body impaled on the sword. I knew it wouldn't hold her for long though, but I was already in motion. With shifter strength, I shoved her toward the portal, and heaved Morningstar out of her back as she fell into Void.

The other Furies screamed in response, and the alligator roared, "You dare betray us like this?"

She ambled toward me with unnatural speed, her jaws wide, her fangs glistening under the moonlight, and I knew she would chomp down on me within seconds. But then Belial lunged at her with a growl, picking her up with his impossible strength. He lifted the alligator over his head and swung her around like he was a wrestler, before tossing her into the portal. Yes! Two Furies down, one to go. But we had to make it quick, before the Furies came through again.

I turned toward Belial, hoping he would see in my eyes that this had been my plan all along and that I hadn't betrayed him—but before I could so much as say his name, something rammed into me from the side. I fell down the stairs, landing badly on an unconscious bear shifter, while Morningstar fell out of my hand.

The third Fury, still a cloud of noxious, yellow gas that radiated rage, hovered over me like a malevolent cloud. "My sisters told me about you," the rattling, wheezing voice said. "They said you wanted vengeance, and I will give it to you. All you have to do is let me in, and we can have our retribution together."

Her power surged into me, filling me with rage, hatred, and a need for revenge, but this time I fought back against it. I reached for the mate bond with Belial and focused on that. "No," I forced out through clenched teeth. "I'm done with vengeance. It won't change the past, and I have to move forward."

The Fury hissed above me, and her incorporeal body

reached for me. "You will be mine," she snapped, as she surged toward me.

I blasted her with ice as I scrambled back, but it did little against her ghostly form. She surrounded me suddenly, and I coughed, blinking and trying to fight as my vision turned completely yellow. I was being smothered, like she had wrapped herself around me like some demented snake, and I fought against it with everything I had. I closed my eyes and imagined ice coming out of every pore of my body, adrenaline sending my power shooting through me like lightning, and the next moment I was free.

The Fury screamed, blown apart by my ice. I quickly shifted into wolf form and ran, heading back toward the portal. We had to get her inside it somehow. I stopped just in front of the portal and returned to human form, while the Fury coalesced into a spirit again a few feet away from me. She dove to attack me, but something long and black wrapped around her, pulling her back.

Belial stood behind her, and chains made of darkness suddenly burst out of him and wrapped around the Fury. He pummeled her with his magic as the shadow chains wrapped around her, trapping her inside.

"You!" she screamed, struggling to get free. I added my own ice around her, reinforcing Belial's magic, but it was obvious it couldn't hold her for long. The Fury was too strong.

Belial met my eyes, and a sudden calm came over his face, as though he'd made a decision. He rushed toward the Void portal, dragging the shrieking Fury with him. She

broke free enough to latch onto him, the two of them struggling against each other, as he leaped toward the portal.

"Belial!" I screamed as he fell into the portal along with
the Fury, and I desperately reached out to him. He extended
a hand, as if he wanted to caress my face one last time, but I
grabbed tightly onto it. For a moment, I thought I was going
to be pulled in to the portal as well, and screamed with a
new kind of rage.

Belial's hand started slipping through mine and I
gripped on tighter, reaching into the portal to try and find
his wrist with my other hand. Piercing needles pulled at my
skin, as though the portal was trying to tear me apart atom
by atom, but I refused to let go. I grabbed hold of Belial and
dragged him toward me, until finally, my own hands
reappeared.

Belial pushed himself out of the portal with a growl, and
together we stumbled back a few feet. Belial turned to me,
running his hands over my body as if to check and make sure
I was okay, and then looked back at the chaotic, maddening
swirl of colors and darkness.

"Do you still have the Void key?" he asked.

I nodded, grabbing it from the pocket I'd somehow
managed to stash it inside. "Right here."

"Close the portal, quickly."

I nodded and held the key out, focusing on shutting the
portal down. Opening it hadn't been any different from
using a Faerie key, but closing it proved to be harder. The
portal was like a door in the wind, fighting against my every
attempt to shut it, and I could hear the echo of the Furies'

voices on the other side. Belial reached over and rested his hand upon mine, adding his strength, and together we wrestled the portal closed.

All at once, it was silent. The overwhelming urge to join the Furies went away like it had never existed at all. The shifters and imps, who had been passed out throughout the courtyard, all seemed to wake up at once and looked around themselves in horror. There was some confusion and shouting, but screams of rage turned to whimpers of fear and panic as most of them started running away, as if they were terrified. Belial released his undead at the same time, and they collapsed in a heap, then turned to dust and floated away on the breeze.

I rushed toward Belial and threw myself into his arms before he could say anything. He embraced me tightly, burying his face in my hair and breathing me in, like he couldn't believe we were really still together.

"I thought you were going to send me to Void too," Belial said, his arms tightening around me.

"Don't be an idiot," I said, pulling back and punching him in the arm lightly. "I was only doing it to trick them."

"I figured that out eventually, but you could have warned me. That was reckless."

"*You're* one to talk," I added, punching him again for good measure. A little harder this time. "You were going to sacrifice yourself to save me."

"I couldn't let that Fury possess you. I know all too well there are costs to being an Elder God, and I wouldn't wish the same fate on you."

"But I almost lost you."

"It would have been worth it anyway, knowing you were safe." He took my face in his hands and gazed into my eyes. "I would do anything for you, Eira. There's no point in life without you. I love you."

My heart swelled as I looked at him. "I love you too."

"Does that mean you're done trying to kill me?" he asked, arching an eyebrow.

"Yes, I'm done with that. I've realized vengeance isn't the answer." I cocked my head to the side with a wry grin. "But don't piss me off or I might change my mind again."

"Noted, my mate," he said with a short laugh, before sweeping me into his arms and kissing me hard.

A low growl made us break apart and turn around. "Mate?" Skoll asked, his voice disgusted.

My brothers, still in wolf form, both watched us with fury in their eyes, but it was a pissed off look I recognized. They were no longer under the Furies' control, but they'd also just seen me kissing the man who had killed our father.

"Yes, Belial is my mate," I said, taking his hand and facing my brothers. "I know you might find that hard to accept, but there's no denying it."

Skoll and Hati exchanged a glance, and then Hati said, "We will talk about this later."

The two of them dashed off down the courtyard and disappeared the same way the other shifters and imps had gone. I had a feeling family dinners would be uncomfortable for a while, but at least they weren't controlled by the Furies anymore. They might never accept Belial as my mate, but I'd do my best to convince them he wasn't our enemy. I didn't want to choose my mate over my family, but there was no denying this bond between us anymore.

We would be mates for the rest of our lives—and mine felt like it was just beginning.

22

BELIAL

"——And then I pulled his dumb ass out of the portal," Eira said, tossing the rest of her drink back.

The chatter of the bar surrounded us, cocooning us in as we sat at the counter. We'd returned here after leaving the Ursuline Convent, and we'd both agreed we could use a good drink after everything we'd just gone through.

Yumi blinked a few times, looking between us with her mouth agape. "So you saved him? Wow. And here I thought the almighty Lord of Death could get himself out of any situation."

I scowled at them both and finished off my drink too. "I could have handled it."

"Yeah, sure." Eira rolled her eyes, before finishing off the story with how she'd closed the portal, trapping the Furies in Void.

"That's one crazy tale," Yumi said, as she poured us

another drink. "I'm just glad that New Orleans is safe again."

"You and me both," I said.

Yumi's eyes suddenly widened at something behind me, and I turned, readying to defend my bar if there was a threat. When I saw who had her spooked, I released my magic with a sigh. Loki was a threat, but not in that way.

Tonight his black hair was slicked back and he wore a tuxedo with an emerald green bow tie and matching emerald cuff links, as if he'd just arrived from some fancy charity ball. He flashed us a dazzling, impish smile. "Hello, friends. I see you've survived the night. How fortuitous."

"No thanks to you." I narrowed my eyes at him. "We could have used your help tonight."

He waved his hand dismissively. "I had other pressing matters to attend to, and it seems you've protected the city just fine on your own. Though I'm surprised you're still here, Belial. I thought Eira would have sent you back to Void by now."

Eira reached over and grabbed my hand. "We've worked out our issues."

"I see that," Loki said, his eyes dropping to our hands and then flicking back up to her face. "What do your brothers have to say about that?"

"I don't think they're thrilled, but they'll just have to get over it. Just like the two of you will need to learn to be civil with each other."

"Not possible," I muttered.

Loki's face shifted to amusement. "Oh, Belial. I'm sure

we can work something out for the sake of our darling Eira, can't we?"

I glanced at Eira, who looked at me with her bright blue eyes so full of hope it was impossible to say no. "Fine. I'll try."

Loki chuckled at that and then turned back to Eira. "Now that your mission to find your brothers and the missing shifters and imps has been successful, what do you plan to do next?"

"I'd like to go back to being a messenger between the fae and the demons," she said. "I miss visiting Faerie and I want to embrace both parts of who I am."

"That's an excellent idea, and I'm sure I can make that happen. I can always use a trusted messenger." His smirk turned on me. "Especially one who can call on some pretty deadly backup when needed. But first, I do believe we had a deal, and it's time for you to pay up."

I glared at his outstretched hand, knowing exactly what he was asking for. "We should have destroyed the damn thing."

"I'm surprised you didn't," Loki said.

"Eira wouldn't let me," I grumbled.

"I swore I wouldn't use it on you," Loki pointed out.

"Yes, but that's the only thing you promised. There are plenty of other things you could do with the key, like trying to send Lucifer to Void and so you can take over Hell as the Demon King."

"Now what would give you that idea?" Loki asked, his

face the picture of innocence. "I would never do such a thing. Lucifer and I are old friends."

"Yeah, but so are we, and I wouldn't trust you not to shove a knife in my back."

"He won't do any of that," Eira said, though she didn't sound entirely convinced. She reached into her pocket and pulled out the glittering black stone, before handing it to Loki. "Here."

"I do appreciate you retrieving this for me." Loki's grin widened as his fingers clasped around the Void key. Then the key vanished, disappearing in a swirl of Loki's illusion magic. "I'll contact you soon about your new position."

Then I blinked, and he was gone. No one else in the bar seemed to notice, which made me wonder if he'd concealed himself from all the other patrons the entire time.

"He is a bit dramatic," Eira admitted.

"You act like he's harmless, but I know better." I tossed the rest of my drink back, and Yumi immediately refilled it. I nodded my thanks to her. "He's going to cause more chaos. That's what he does."

"He's not bad," Eira said. "He even helped us, in his own way."

I wasn't convinced. In fact, the only reason I hadn't challenged Loki was because I did believe he had a soft spot for Eira, and that he would never do anything to hurt her. But if that ever changed? He would face my wrath.

"I'll tell Lucifer to keep an eye on him. Now that he has that Void key, he will surely be plotting to use it."

"Speaking of Lucifer..." Eira started, sounding almost nervous. "When do I get to meet the rest of your family?"

"You want to meet them?" I asked, pausing with my drink halfway to my mouth.

"Of course. I already met one of your brothers, but I know you have more siblings, and I'd like to thank your mom again for saving me."

"And Lucifer?" I asked.

She hesitated. "As long as he can forgive me for my father's sins."

"He's forgiven me, by some miracle. I have a feeling he won't blame you for what Fenrir did either."

"Then yes, I'd like to meet him too." She brushed her finger along my jaw. "I'm all in now. Assuming you want me to stay in New Orleans, of course."

"What kind of question is that?" I asked. Wasn't it obvious I was never letting her go?

Before she could answer, I stood up and grabbed her around the waist, then tossed her over my shoulder. She let out a noise of protest, but didn't fight me as I carted her out of the bar, while Yumi rolled her eyes at the two of us.

I carried Eira all the way upstairs to my apartment, and once we were inside, I set her down gently on my bed and knelt in front of her.

"This is your home now," I said, reaching up and cupping her face in my hands. "Or we can get a bigger one if you want. Wherever you want to be, I'll follow. Whenever you're around, the hunger is gone. With you by my side, I won't ever have to feed on the souls of others again. I thought I was soulless, but the truth is, *you're* my soul."

"You're my home, too," she whispered. "I never felt like I had one until I met you."

"I love you so much," I said, sliding my hands down her shoulders. She was so beautiful, and I'd spend the rest of my life showing her just how much she meant to me.

"I love you too," she whispered. She drew me closer, and I leaned into her, pressing myself against her to feel the solidness of her body. I'd already almost lost her, and I wasn't going to let it happen again. She moaned against my mouth as I pulled her hips closer to the edge, rising up so I was level with her. I ground my hard length against her stomach, and she pulled away with a gasp.

"Fuck me," she demanded.

"Gladly," I growled.

We both rid ourselves of our clothes so quickly a human might have blinked and missed it. The need for each other swelled again, as it often did thanks to this mate bond, but this time it was different. We'd almost lost each other tonight, but somehow we'd fought our own inner demons and won the battle, both against the Furies and against our pasts. Together we were ready to move on to whatever came next.

Eira's eyes burned with need as she crawled up the bed and spread her legs invitingly. Her pussy was already gleaming, inviting me in as well. I reached down and dipped my fingers inside, the warm heat of her surrounding me. When I pulled my fingers out, I reached them up to taste her. I closed my eyes, savoring her unique, wonderful flavor. I'd been hungry for so long, but she was the one thing that truly sated me.

"Enough," Eira said, pulling me down. "Fuck me properly."

"As you wish," I said, and flipped her over. She got on all fours, arching her back and pushing her ass back toward me. I grabbed hold of her hips and stilled her, need pounding through me. I rubbed my cock along her pussy, teasing her a bit more until she made a noise of protest, and then slammed inside.

She let out a yelp, grabbing onto the sheets below as she clenched around me, drawing me in deeper. I closed my eyes, savoring the feeling. This felt more like coming home than anything else I'd ever had. Eira was made for me.

I began thrusting, pounding into her so hard I thought it would hurt her. But she just arched her back and begged for more, always goading me into going deeper, faster, to try and consume as much of her as I could. I could never get enough of her, and I wanted *more*. I leaned over her, not slowing my pace at all, and nosed at her neck. She smelled intoxicating, and I licked and bit at her skin until she turned her head and offered me her lips. She reached up with one hand and pulled me closer, somehow sliding me deeper inside of her.

"Yes," she moaned as she drove herself back on my dick once more. I bit the shell of her ear.

"Mine," I murmured as I pistoned my hips into her. She let out a little noise with each thrust, raising in intensity. She was already trembling around me, moments away from coming. I loved how responsive her body was. I looked forward to spending all my nights trying to draw every noise out of her.

There's time enough for that, I thought as she clenched around me, her voice going hoarse as she started coming. I pulled back to watch her entire body lose control, pleasure overtaking me as well. I held on longer, wanting to push her to the limits of however much pleasure she could take.

She shuddered, tightening around me, drawing me closer and closer to that edge. Finally, with a growl, I let it consume me. My movements slowed, and my vision went white with the force of my climax. I drove myself in one last time and emptied myself into her. She gasped, body still quaking with the aftereffects of her own orgasm.

When we collapsed onto the bed together, I pulled Eira to me immediately. She turned in my arms and nestled up against me, putting her head on my chest. We were both panting hard, and I knew that this was just the beginning. I wanted to fuck her into oblivion until the sun rose, but for now, I was content to just hold her.

She hummed happily as she draped her arm over my hip and pulled me even closer to her. When I smiled down at her, she looked back up at me, eyes glinting happily in the dim light of my bedroom. She really was my home, my fated mate, my everything. *Mine.*

23

EIRA

I looked up at the imposing black doors of Lucifer's palace in Hell, and then back at Belial, swallowing hard. It was a week after the battle with the Furies, and Belial had wanted to take me to meet his father as soon as possible. But nothing would have prepared me for this.

Lucifer's palace was in Hell in the equivalent of Earth's Egypt and looked like something that had been built around the same time as the pyramids, with huge columns covered in ivy and flowers that glowed in the night. A few sections of the palace were under construction, adding a startlingly modern contradiction to the ancient structure.

I'd never been to Hell before, since I'd been born in Faerie and raised on Earth. Most younger demons never had, not since Lucifer had ended the war with the angels, and he and Archangel Michael closed off Heaven and Hell and moved all the angels and demons to Earth. At the time, the two realms had been completely decimated and unable to support life, but now each side was slowly working to rebuild their homes. Starting with this palace.

Hell was completely different from how I'd pictured it too. Hell was the realm of eternal night, just like Heaven was the land of never ending day. An endless black sky stretched overhead, sparkling with countless stars and the thin sliver of the moon. There was no fire and brimstone, and instead it was quite chilly, not that the temperature bothered me, of course.

Belial glanced over at me, his jaw clenched so hard it looked painful. "I haven't been here since I tried to over-throw my father. It's...strange being back."

"You'll be fine," I said, taking his hand. "The past is in the past, remember?"

"Yes, but the past is long when you're immortal." He looked down at our intertwined hands with a scowl, but let me lead him to the entrance of the palace.

Before we could reach the huge doors, they suddenly flew open, and a toddler with wings—one black, one white—rode out on a three-headed dog. She laughed as she held the dog's collar like reigns and directed him forward. Then the girl caught sight of Belial and let out an ungodly shriek.

"Bel Bel!" She flung herself off of the dog and flew right into Belial's arms, her little wings flapping against the cool night air.

Belial laughed and caught her, spinning her around like this was completely normal. I'd never seen such joy on his face before, and she looked back at him with the same adora-tion. He was like a completely different person, and I knew this must be his sister, Aurora. The one he'd sacrificed his soul to save. The love they shared was unmistakable.

The three-headed dog nudged my hand, sniffing at me, and I tried not to panic. As I held very still, trying to see what he would think of me, his tail started wagging, and six eyes looked up at me, imploring. I tentatively reached out to pat his head. He wagged harder, and began bouncing circles around me. I let out a startled laugh, looking back over at Belial. This definitely hadn't been the welcome wagon I'd expected, but it was much better than anything I'd had in mind.

Belial grinned and set the girl down. "Eira, this is my sister Aurora, and the family dog Cerberus."

"It's nice to meet you both," I said.

"Aurora?" another voice called from inside. A beautiful woman with long blond hair and the face of an angel—literally—emerged from the palace, then relaxed when she saw Aurora was with us. "There you are. I see you've found your brother."

"Bel Bel!" Aurora said with a grin.

"I'm so glad you're here," Hannah said, as she embraced her son. I'd seen her once before while in Faerie, when she sacrificed herself and became the 3rd Horseman, Famine. She was just as impressive now, wearing a silver crown and a shimmering blue dress. Flowers grew at her feet, as if her very presence inspired them to rise up, and she glowed faintly as she moved. She had once been Eve, and then Persephone, and dozens of other lives throughout all of time, but now she was in the body of an angel for her final life.

Her long love affair with Lucifer across countless centuries was both tragic and romantic, from what Belial had told me of it.

"You must be Eira," she said, smiling warmly at me. "It's lovely to meet you properly. Please come inside."

She beckoned us inside before we could have a chance to say no, and practically shoved Belial through the doors when he hesitated. I hid a smile as I followed them inside.

"We've spent the last few months restoring the palace here, and it's finally coming together now," Hannah said, as she led us through a grand hall with giant columns circled by vines and impossibly tall ceilings. Windows and high doorways cut through the roof and the higher portions of the walls, allowing winged demons to move in and out of the hall freely without stopping to land. Flowers that glowed with a soft blue light grew from every corner, and a large fountain in the middle of the hall was full of luminous fish.

"It's...much more alive than I thought it would be," I said.

"My mother has what you'd call a green thumb," Belial said. "A remnant of her time as Persephone."

I nodded, putting it all together in my head. Persephone had been a fae of the Spring Court, and was Damien's mother. Would Belial's flirty half-fae brother be here tonight?

As we continued walking, Aurora babbled excitedly at Belial in toddler speak, but I could only make out a few of her words. He seemed to understand though, or at least pretended he did, and seeing him interact with Aurora made my heart melt a little more. She was the reason he'd become Death, when he'd sacrificed himself to save her. I'd been so very wrong about him at first, but now it was so obvious to me how bright his heart was.

Hannah continued telling us about different renovations to the palace as she led us further inside, and each room was more impressive than the last, even the ones under construction. Finally she took us into a dinning room that was a lot less grand than some of the other rooms we'd been in, and I realized it was a more private space, reserved for just her family.

Damien was there, and he flashed us a charming smile when he saw us, but my eyes quickly looked past him to the other two men he stood with. My breath caught at the sight of Lucifer, who shared many of the same features as Belial but had a more refined air to him. While Belial was all tattoos and t-shirts, Lucifer wore an exquisitely made black suit and every inch of him, from his dark stubble to the silver crown on his head, was the picture of perfection. He was the kind of man who turned heads when he entered a room without even trying, and when he turned his eyes on me, my heart nearly stopped.

But then Lucifer smiled, and I could breathe again, because I saw only warmth in his eyes. He wasn't going to smite me down right here for being a part of my father's rebellion. I knew he could do it too, since he not only had all of his original powers, but also those of the 2nd Horseman, War.

Lucifer turned toward Belial with open arms. "Belial. So good to see you again."

Belial's eyes narrowed, as if expecting a trick, but he put Aurora down and reluctantly embraced his father. He took a deep breath in, and his shoulders relaxed a tiny bit, before he stepped back. "It's good to be back."

Lucifer smiled and patted him on the back, before looking over at me. "And this must be your mate."

"This is Eira," Belial said, motioning for me to come forward.

"An honor, my king." I dipped my head in deference to Lucifer, and then wondered if I should bow instead.

To my surprise, Lucifer took my hand and kissed the back of it. "Anyone who has tamed my son is most welcome here," he said, his eyes twinkling.

"I'm not sure he can ever be truly tamed," I said with a smile.

"You've come closer than anyone else though," the other man said with a grin.

I'd temporarily forgotten his presence in the wake of Lucifer's attention, but now I turned toward him. This man looked almost identical to Lucifer, and was so obviously his son that I could only stare at him in amazement. He looked like Belial too, and even a bit like Aurora and Damien. The family resemblance between all of the siblings was strong, and tied them all back to their father.

"I'm Kassiel, Belial's youngest brother," he said with a grin. "Damien has told me all about you."

"Don't worry, only good things," Damien said, winking at me. "I'm just glad you two finally came to your senses."

"I suspect she had to bash him over the head with a rock to get that to happen," Kassiel said with a laugh.

"No, but I did impale him with an ice spear one time," I told them.

"Ooh, I like this one," Lucifer said, as he clasped Belial on the shoulder.

Belial rolled his eyes, but he didn't move away either, and I had a feeling things between him and his father would be repaired a tiny bit more tonight. They had a long and difficult history spanning centuries, but I was confident that things were going to change going forward. *After all, he has me now.*

Hannah announced that dinner was ready, and we all sat down at a long table, where an assortment of glasses and fancy dishes lay arranged in front of us. Belial pulled my chair out for me, and I smiled at him as I took my seat.

As soon as we were all settled, the wine glasses all filled, as if by magic. I picked up my glass with a grin. "I'm liking this place more and more."

"Blame Damien for that trick," Belial said with a snort as he grabbed his own glass. "God of wine and all."

"I don't see you complaining," Damien said.

Lucifer stood, raising his own glass. "I would like to propose a toast." Everyone quieted down and he continued, smiling at all of his family members seated around him, from ancient Belial to baby Aurora. "If there is one thing I have learned in all my many years, it's that family is everything.

I'm so happy to have all of you here tonight, including the newest member of our family, Eira." He motioned toward me with a mischievous grin. "I truly hope you can keep Belial in line, because I'd really hate to have to exile him again."

Everyone around the table laughed, while Belial shook his head. "My rebellious days are over." He took my hand in his own and gazed into my eyes. "I've found my place now."

Hannah practically beamed at these words, looking over at Belial with pride, before turning back to the others. "Now that Kassiel and Belial have both found their mates, it's time for Damien to find his mate too, don't you think?"

Damien waved her away. "You know I have no interest in settling down."

"He'll surely run out of eligible men and women soon," Kassiel said with a laugh. "If he hasn't found his mate yet, he must not have one."

Damien smiled devilishly over his wine. "Or maybe one man or woman will never be enough for me."

"Love is not the kind of thing you can predict or control," Hannah said to her son with amusement in her eyes. "Someday it might surprise you."

Lucifer reached over and took Hannah's hand. "It certainly continues to surprise me, even after all these years."

"Hey, if it can happen for me, it can happen for anyone," Belial said.

"And sometimes with the person you least expect," I replied, gazing back at him with the full force of my love.

"To family!" Lucifer said, and everyone raised their glasses and toasted.

I kept my eyes on Belial as we clinked our glasses together and drank, and I saw my love reflected back at me.

After years of feeling as though I never belonged anywhere, I'd found my place too—right here beside Death.

ABOUT THE AUTHOR

Elizabeth Briggs is the *New York Times* bestselling author of paranormal and fantasy romance. She graduated from UCLA with a degree in Sociology and has worked for an international law firm, mentored teens in writing, and volunteered with dog rescue groups. Now she's a full-time geek who lives in Los Angeles with her family and a pack of fluffy dogs.

Visit Elizabeth's website: www.elizabethbriggs.net

Join Elizabeth's Facebook group for fun book chat and early sneak peeks!

Made in United States
North Haven, CT
17 September 2022

24236677R00125